#minithology

FAIRIES IN JARS

EDITED BY   N.D. GRAY

featuring

TRACY EIRE   ELIZABETH KNOLLSTON   EMBER FANE

KARLI STITES   HEIDI MOONE

CONTENTS

INTRODUCTION

ONE OF THE GREATEST PLEASURES of heading up an anthology is creating the theme. The brainstorming can be quite fun. However, this #minithology's theme came not in a flurry of thoughts but in a daydream.

I was thinking of lightning bugs. How much I miss them, living here in the desert as I do. How, as children, we would catch them and put them in a jar.

For a moment, my feet were bare and buried in thick Ohio grass, cool in the dark of the evening. The glass of the Mason jar was also cool. And smooth.

The firefly lights were lazy. They winked on. And off. Here. Then, there.

While a slight summer breeze tickled over my long hair, I ran through the cool grass, my skirts brushing against my knees. The scent of things growing filled every lungful of happy air. With careful hands, I caught a light and dropped the bug into the jar. Screwed the lid on. Lifted the jar to my nose so I could peer inside.

What if... a fairy had looked back at me?

My childhood would have been vastly more interesting, for starters.

In the world of stories, there are many fairies. Good, bad, and indifferent. Whether we love them or hate them, we find them fascinating, as the Cottingley Fairies proved. And what if we should stumble upon a fairy in a jar? How fascinated would we be then? How curious? What circumstances led it there? Did it need to escape? Or is the jar shelter?

In this #minithology, five exceptional authors have crafted five amazing stories. So, sit out on the deck with a glass of lemonade. Watch the fireflies wink on, one by one. Then, read about the lives of our fairies in jars.

ND Gray
May 2021
Camp Verde, AZ

Our Fairy of Mischief and Chaos has penned a story about an atypical fairy godmother. Drakonae do not think of fairies as sentient—if they ever think of them at all. When one fairy is captured and gifted to a young Drakonae girl, she fears the worst. Can two unlikely friends bridge the gap between species and bring change to their world?

THE LIGHT OF MERIGOLD
A PRELUDE TO SKYFIRE
Karli Stites

BLUEBELL

MEMORIES WERE FICKLE THINGS. At times, they broke our hearts, leeching the color from the world until nothing remained. But the further I flew from my home, the more my memories started to twist and change into something unrecognizable. Was I wrong about my family? Maybe it wasn't too late. Maybe I *could* be a fairy they could be proud of. Someone they could love.

No. Keep going. They hurt you. They rejected you.

I sighed, slumping in the air while my iridescent gossamer wings continued fluttering in the warm summer breeze. My body stilled for a moment over a gorgeous yellow flower, but I barely spared it a glance before I moved on. As a music fairy, it felt almost unnatural for me to be depressed, especially while I floated in the air with the tinkling wind flowing around me. But I couldn't help it. I'd officially left my family. I'd left the entire fairy world behind.

"Not like they'll even notice I'm gone," I muttered. I tried not to wallow in my misery. I didn't want to. Fairies weren't meant to be sad, after all. Happy, loyal, proud, cunning, and vengeful—when the need arose—but never sad.

I never set out to be a disappointment, but I couldn't help the way I was born. I couldn't help the fact that I, Bluebell of the Elemental Fairies, was born a music fairy. My family had developed quite a reputation of birthing strong elemental fairies—those with power over earth, air, fire, and water. When I was born, blue-skinned, blue-eyed, and blue-haired, my parents were convinced I would be a strong water fairy. But they were wrong. And they didn't let me forget it.

I straightened my shoulders, steeling myself against the onslaught of memories that threatened to weigh me down. Memories *were* fickle at times, but I knew what I had to do. My family didn't deserve me. I didn't know where I was going, but anywhere had to be better than where I came from.

When I started to smell something unusual, I stopped. Landing softly on a nearby leaf, I lifted my nose to the sky and tried to categorize the new scent.

"Dragon fire," I whispered.

Where the hell was I? I'd never ventured so far from home before. Ever since I was a young fairy, I was told to stay away from the Drakonae. We might have lived on Drakon together, but we certainly weren't friends. As far as I knew, they didn't even think fairies were intelligent beings. The Fairy Council seemed to think it was better that way, but I wasn't too sure. Fairies were very closed-off in general, but we made an effort to make contact with the other species living on Drakon—all except the Drakonae apparently.

"Not my problem," I whispered.

But this is my problem.

I didn't know where I was, but it was obvious that I was close to a Drakonae clan. One of the fire clans. I was equal parts grateful and annoyed that the Fairy Council had never reached out to the Drakonae. Since they didn't think we were intelligent, any wandering Drakonae that saw me would probably ignore me. Although, if we'd had a working relationship with them, I would be able to get some help. It was a double-edged sword I supposed.

"Focus, Bluebell."

I obviously couldn't stay near a Drakonae clan. Although... It *would* be nice to see people. Maybe I could even sneak some food. Fairies only ate fruit and vegetables, and we usually foraged for everything, but I imagined the Drakonae had some interesting dishes. I definitely wanted to try some of that. And they would certainly have some beautiful lakes and streams around here to wash up in.

But I really shouldn't.

It was a bad idea.

Really bad.

BLUEBELL

A MONTH LATER, I WAS settling into my new life on the outskirts of the Drakonae clan I'd made my new home. It only took a few days to figure out it was the Skyfire clan. The Drakonae were very traditional; everyone in the clan lived there because they had a specific power *and* a specific scale color. Everyone in the Skyfire clan had sky blue hair and when they transformed, their dragons were a gorgeous sky blue as well.

I knew I'd made the right choice to stay when I saw the first Drakonae with hair that perfectly matched mine. Obviously, they didn't have the same blue skin as me—fire Drakonae all had tan skin—but I felt a kinship with them that made me happier than I'd been in a long time. I found myself humming while I flew around, tending to flowers around the outskirts of the city. As I did, I saw the effects of my music slowly transform the mood of anyone who happened to be near me.

Music might not have been an elemental power, but it was powerful in its own right. I could influence the mood and feelings of those around me with my voice. Even though I was a social outcast back home, I was always very popular at parties. Every fairy wanted me to sing for them and I was all too happy to oblige, thinking it would make them like me more. It never worked though, because they were only using me.

Laughing at my old life, I continued humming a happy new tune I'd composed last week. I hadn't written any words to it, but I had a feeling they would come to me soon. I flew to the next meadow to check on the flowers I'd planted a few days ago. I didn't know why, but I'd felt a pull to this place that refused to be denied. Looking down, I noticed they had started to sprout. I reached down and touched the soil. It was wet. Someone was taking care of my flowers!

"Unusual," I murmured.

I looked around, wary that someone was watching me, but I didn't notice anything. I flew around the meadow, cautiously checking to make sure it was empty.

When I was convinced I was alone, I started to sing the low melodic song that I'd used on all my flowers. I was no earth fairy, but I had a few tricks up my sleeve. I'd woven a song together years ago that encouraged flowers to grow and it worked fabulously. My family had always thought I just had a green thumb, and I'd had no inclination to convince them otherwise.

Almost immediately after I finished the last notes of my song, the sprouts grew a little higher. I smiled.

I started to fly away when I heard a scream. I didn't even think, I just flew. Darting towards the scream—which I was certain was a young girl—I abandoned my flowers and ventured toward the front of the meadow, a place I had yet to explore. The closer I got, the more *fire* I smelled. Dragon fire. I was close to Drakonae. There was a reason why I hadn't left the edge of the meadow, but my own safety didn't seem important anymore.

I skidded to a stop right before I entered open space. I needed to analyze the situation first. Hiding behind a large plant, I peered out, my large blue eyes going wide at the scene in front of me. There were two children, a boy and a girl. They both had light blue hair, like all Drakonae in the Skyfire clan. I wasn't too sure how old they were, but I guessed they were between seven and ten. I couldn't tell what color the boy's eyes were, but the girl's eyes shone a golden color so bright I could see it from a distance.

I let out a tiny gasp, shocked by their purity. She cocked her head and I almost thought she heard me, but quickly dismissed it when she returned her attention to the boy standing in front of her.

"Stop, Paxton." She glared at him with an intensity that seemed unusual for her age.

"Stop what, Merigold?" Paxton taunted. *Merigold.* The name fit her. It was a beautiful name for a beautiful young girl.

I could have sworn that I saw her take a deep breath. I wanted to laugh. It was such an adult move.

"Stop chasing me around. Please, Paxton. I'm busy." Merigold smiled and it was like sunshine. I noticed that Paxton wasn't immune, but he was stubborn.

"What are you busy with, Mer? I want to hangout, like we used to."

"I'm tending to my flowers, Pax," Merigold responded. I wasn't surprised that she was the one who had taken care of my sprouts. "And I need to think before the Bonding Ceremony. It's in ten days."

I raised an eyebrow. If her ceremony was that soon, it meant she was only eight years old. Merigold was certainly an anomaly. *Like me.*

"What do you mean? You aren't even bonding; your Warriors are." Paxton sighed. "Why are you worried? You know I'll be one of your Warriors."

"I know, it's not that. But, what about the Drakoni? They're living in the Crystal Mountains, right? They're probably perfectly happy. It's their home. What gives us the right to go in there and make them bond with our Warriors? It's not fair."

My mouth dropped open. She *definitely* didn't sound like she was a child.

"Mer, we've talked about this. You can't talk like that. You'll get into trouble," Paxton chastised.

"I know." Merigold looked around sighed in relief when she didn't see any-one. "I'm sorry. I'll stop."

But I saw the sparkle in her eye that said her words were a lie—she would never stop.

BLUEBELL

OVER THE NEXT FEW DAYS, I kept returning to the meadow, hoping to catch a glimpse of Merigold again. I wasn't sure what it was about her that intrigued me. She was special, I was sure of it. I could tell that she was different than everyone else in the Skyfire clan. Maybe even all of the Drakonae. I liked that.

Four days after I'd first seen Merigold and Paxton, I was singing in the meadow when I saw a shadow creeping near the leaf where I was resting. I immediately perked up, imagining meeting Merigold, who I felt a connection to. Never before had I met a Drakonae, but there was a first time for everything.

It was too late when I realized the shadow was too big to be a young child. Too late when I realized that gentle Merigold would never sneak up on me. Too late when I heard the rough whisper of the Drakonae male who'd trapped me in his grasp.

"You're mine now, little fairy."

MERIGOLD

"MERIGOLD, I HAVE A SURPRISE for you," my father's gruff voice called to me from the doorway.

I lifted my head, eyeing him from where I sat in the library of our estate. It wasn't unusual for him to get me presents, especially since my mother had died a year ago. I figured it was his way of trying to connect with me.

"What is it, father?" I tried to sound excited, but I really wasn't. My father didn't have a clue what I was interested in and some of his previous gifts had been... unusual. To be honest, gifts made me uncomfortable, and I would have preferred it if he spent time with me.

"If I told you, it wouldn't be a surprise," he pointed out. That was true, but I didn't like surprises. I constantly reminded my father of that, but he ignored it.

I sighed, following him out of the library. I preferred to be surrounded by books if I wasn't out in the meadow tending to the flowers. None of the younger Drakonae kids understood, but that's what I liked to do, so why would I pretend?

My father walked me down the hallway and into the sleeping quarters. The hallways were sky blue, like the color of our hair. We continued walking in silence until we reached an ornate golden door. My room. I wasn't happy that he'd gone into my room without asking—a girl needed her privacy, even if she was only eight years old—but I didn't say anything. I wasn't one for conflict.

He pushed into my room without asking. I wasn't surprised. Lord Rolark Skyfire didn't ask for anything; he demanded, and then he took what he wanted.

"Here it is!" He gestured with a flourish.

I looked around my room, but it looked the same as always. The same color scheme that dominated my life: creamy white walls, golden-framed bed, sky blue bedding. One wall filled with bookshelves. An armoire filled with all the latest fashions. A sitting area with a comfortable couch, two small chairs, and a coffee table. My eyes passed quickly over the bathroom door as they came to a stop on the last piece of furniture. This time, I spotted something new. Because sitting on my wooden desk was something that wasn't there before.

I inched closer, curious to see what my father had brought me. It was a cylindrical shape, short and made of glass. It looked like... a jar?

"Is that a jar?"

My father huffed. "There's obviously something inside of it."

I continued walking closer, giving the jar a second look. From my current position, it looked empty, but I knew my father wouldn't have given me an empty jar. When I finally reached my desk, I peered into the jar, and my eyebrows scrunched together when I saw a small blue thing at the bottom of the jar. I was about to speak when it moved. *Wow!*

The tiny creature, which had been asleep, awoke suddenly. It lifted its head, looking around with wide blue eyes, before realizing it was trapped. I saw those same pretty blue eyes—a slightly darker shade than my own hair—widen in shock and then water. I felt a pang in my chest. How could my father do such a thing?

"See?" My father pointed to the poor creature proudly. "It's beautiful, isn't it? She reminded me of you."

I wasn't happy, but I didn't want him to know that I rejected his gift. The creature was safer with me. "What is she? Are you sure she's okay in there?"

"A fairy. I found her flying around in our meadow. Don't worry, Merigold. Fairies aren't intelligent beings. She won't even notice a thing, I'm sure. But she will sing for you. I know you love to sing. This one has a pretty voice."

Fairies! I couldn't believe it. I'd heard about them, of course, but they never came near the Drakonae. I wondered why this one was so close to the Skyfire clan. I also sincerely doubted my father's claim that fairies weren't intelligent. Especially considering the way the tiny blue fairy's eyes fumed when he spoke.

"Are you sure, father?"

His eyes narrowed. "Of course, I'm sure. If you don't want her, I'll take her myself. I could use some music in my own quarters."

The fairy's eyes looked panicked at his suggestion and I was sure mine mirrored hers. "No! I want her. Definitely. I love my present. Thank you, father."

He nodded, then smiled. "Good." He turned and walked towards the door. "Don't forget you have lessons tomorrow."

"Of course not. Thank you. Goodnight." The door closed and then he was gone. And I was alone with the fairy.

BLUEBELL

"I'M SO SORRY," SHE BLURTED out immediately after her father left. I resisted the urge to raise my eyebrows. I didn't want her to know how intelligent I actually was, although I had the feeling she was already in on the secret.

After waking up in a *freaking jar*, I wasn't a happy fairy. The Drakonae man was smart, though. I could have easily escaped from a cage, either by squeezing through the bars or with my voice. I didn't know what to think about Merigold. She was innocent in my kidnapping, but I was still at her mercy.

"Really, I am. I can tell you're skeptical." She leaned forward. "I've always been told that fairies aren't intelligent, but I think that's a lie. You seem plenty smart to me. I'm sure you could teach me a lot about Drakon, actually."

She was right about that. Fairies were naturally nosy; we knew everyone's business. Since I was a natural outcast, I'd taken the initiative to spend more time exploring Drakon, meeting new creatures along the way. Merigold wouldn't believe the things I'd seen.

"I'm Merigold." She smiled widely. "You're very pretty. I've never met a fairy before, so I'm not sure what to call you. I get that you don't want to talk to me, though. My father *did* just kidnap you. He's not the nicest. I told him that I didn't want any more presents, but he's pretty insistent. I think he's just not sure what to do with me. My mom died last year. She was nice to me and we had a lot in common. She taught me that everyone and everything on Drakon has a purpose."

The young Drakonae girl with the sky-blue hair and blazing golden eyes leaned forward in her chair. I found myself hovering closer to the front of my jar, hanging on her every word.

"We're all connected. I believe that." She sighed and slumped back in her chair. "That's why I can't believe my father could do something like this. Don't worry, I'll get you out of here."

That time, I didn't hold back my eyebrows.

"I knew it! You *can* understand me." Looking smug and entirely too old for her eight, she smirked. I rolled my eyes. She laughed.

"Well, then. Looks like I have some work to do. I have to prove myself. I want us to be friends, after all, little fairy."

I rolled my eyes again. She was sweet, but I was getting tired of that nickname.

"Bluebell."

"What?" She looked at me with wide eyes, shocked that I'd actually spoken.

"You can call me Bluebell."

MERIGOLD

FAIRIES. WERE. REAL.

Yes, I knew this. Of course I did. We learned about them in school. They were mentioned randomly in stories growing up. But they were so rarely seen, they'd almost reached mythological status. Fairies were tiny pretty things, beautiful magical beings that were there for us to look at—no substance. Not intelligent.

Wrong.

I felt lied to. *If they lied about that, what else were they lying about?* For the next few days, I walked around the estate with a sharp eye. I looked at everyone with suspicion. Sure, I grew up with these people, but did I know them? Did they know the truth or was everyone in the dark? Maybe my mom was right when she told me things weren't right with Drakon. This *had* to be what she was talking about. We couldn't treat living beings like this.

Either way, I needed a plan to help Bluebell escape. Something foolproof. I couldn't let my father or one of his Warriors see me let her out. He wouldn't be happy with me, and there would be consequences. I knew I had to do something before my Bonding Ceremony. After that, I'd barely have any time alone. Once I was assigned two Warriors, it would be their job to follow me everywhere. Pax would make sure to stick to me like glue.

Bluebell and I had discussed a few ideas, but I'd found it difficult to get away with the Bonding so close. Nighttime was my new favorite time of day. I loved Drakon—truly adored it with all my heart—and Bluebell had travelled all over. She'd spent years meeting new people, living in new environments, discovering new plants, and going on adventures. I'd never met anyone like her before. Each night when my eyes finally became too heavy for me to keep open, she'd sing me a lullaby, and it was always the prettiest song I'd ever heard.

I hadn't been so happy since my mother had died, but I knew I needed to help set her free, so I kept searching for a way.

The answer finally came to me the day before my Bonding Ceremony.

"Bluebell," I whispered, running up to her jar in my room. I'd taken to letting her out each night so she could stretch her wings and fly around, but she had to stay in the jar during the day in case someone visited my room unexpectedly.

"Hello, Merigold," Bluebell responded in her musical voice. I'd learned over the past five days that she was usually very cheerful. Although, she did get into snarky moods sometimes. I liked those, too, though. It always made me giggle when she got all fired up.

"I think I found our big break!" I whooped.

"How so?" She looked skeptical.

"Well, my Bonding Ceremony is tomorrow, right?"

Bluebell nodded. "Yes, of course."

"Basically, everyone is freaking out. Last minute preparations and everything. We have to travel to the Crystal Mountains. It's not too far, but there's no telling how long we'll be there. Some Drakonae take longer than others to bond with Drakoni. First, we have to get to the mountains. Then, we have to find Drakoni. And *then,* we have to find Drakoni willing to bond. *And then,* we have to make sure those willing Drakoni are actually compatible. Sounds like a lot, right? Well, it is. So, they're doing a lot right now. And my Warriors are reviewing the Bonding Oath. Lots of things are happening. I think we can take advantage of this craziness. We'll just slip out into the meadow and I'll let you out. It'll be easy!"

My fairy friend wasn't impulsive. She thought things through. This time was no different. She spent several minutes thinking over my plan. I thought it was pretty good. Especially for an eight-year-old. I waited in silence for her answer.

She smiled. "It's a good plan, Merigold. Well done."

I cheered. "Yes!"

"Just remember that it might not be as easy as you think. We should be careful. I don't want you to get in trouble with your father." Her tiny nose scrunched up when she mentioned my father.

"Don't worry, it'll be fine. I promise," I reassured her.

BLUEBELL

THE PAST FIVE DAYS WITH Merigold had been more fun than I wanted to admit. Luckily, she was the only one around, so I didn't have to admit it to anyone. I didn't realize how unhappy I was, how lost I'd felt until I'd met her. *And now I was leaving.*

Somehow, it felt wrong. I remembered the kinship I'd felt with Merigold when I first saw her and the connection that formed when we met, growing as we spent more time together. She felt like someone I was meant to protect. She was special. Like the Drakoni, fairies were linked to Old Magic. The Drakoni were the first inhabitants of Drakon, but fairies weren't too far behind. I had a feeling that I was supposed to meet Merigold Skyfire, and as a being of Old Magic, I should trust those feelings.

But how would that even work? Fairies were supposed to stay away from Drakonae. They didn't even think of us as an intelligent species. Not to mention the fact that her father had kidnapped me....

I sighed in my jar, waiting for Merigold to return from her expedition. She was checking the hallways to make sure they were clear before we left for the meadow. Things still didn't feel right, but I wasn't sure what to do. I didn't want to stay locked up forever, but I didn't want to be alone out in the world either.

The door opened and Merigold slipped inside. She tiptoed over to my jar, an unnecessary tactic since we were the only two people in the room. I laughed at her antics. She was also wearing all black, something else that she'd insisted on.

"All clear!"

My gut was churning. I gulped and nodded. "Okay, let's go."

Merigold's smile didn't reach her eyes. She nodded and picked up my jar, carefully hiding me inside of her black jacket "just in case." When I was tucked away, Merigold made her way to the door, peeking outside after she opened it and shut it quietly behind her.

I was curious as we made our way down the hallway, since I had been unconscious the first time I'd made the journey. Fairies tended to live in nature, and I'd never been inside another Drakonae home, so I wasn't sure what to expect. Everything was ornate and decorated with the Skyfire clan's dragon colors. I snorted.

"Not surprised," I muttered.

Merigold looked down at me, confused. When she saw me point to the décor, she laughed.

"Dragons," she explained, shrugging. I rolled my eyes. *Ridiculous.*

We fairies did have our vices, but the Drakonae seemed a little full of themselves sometimes. I'd have to make sure that my Merigold didn't turn out like that. My breath caught when I realized I'd slipped up. I wouldn't be able to do that. Not anymore. I wouldn't be around. That would be someone else's job.

Girl needs a freaking fairy godmother. I took a seat at the bottom of my jar with my arms crossed, pouting like a child. *Crazy dragon shifters.*

Merigold raised an eyebrow at me but didn't comment, familiar with my mood swings. That was another thing I was going to miss about her. She was very understanding.

We only walked a few more minutes before the hallway started to lighten up. Not in paint color—that was the same blue as every other wall in the estate—but I started to see actual daylight. Or, more accurately, the dying light of the setting sun. It matched my mood.

"Success! We're almost there, Bluebell!"

I should have been happy, but the closer we got to our destination, the worse I felt. I touched my forehead. Maybe I had a fever? *No, everything feels normal.*

Then, we were outside. Outside, where I hadn't been in five days. Was I excited? No. I was sad. What was wrong with me?

Merigold walked to the middle of the field. She opened the jar that had held me prisoner for almost a week. I flew out and hovered in front of her, so we were at eye level. Those huge golden eyes that had captivated me from the beginning started to water. Mine followed suit. I couldn't remember the last time I'd actually cried, but my parting with Merigold was sure to end in tears.

"I'm going to miss you, Bluebell," Merigold began. She sniffled and started to cry a little. "I've never met anyone like you before. I've been so lost and sad since my mom died, but you've helped me heal these past few days. I know that my father stole you, and I'm so sorry. You didn't deserve that. You deserve to be free. I hope that you know I never wanted this to happen to you. I hope you don't hold this against me, and you can forgive me for the part I played in your kidnapping. I'll always carry everything that you taught me. You and my mom both convinced me that Drakon needs help. I *know* I can do it. I'll dedicate my life to protecting and fighting for those that can't fight for themselves. You've taught me that and I'm so grateful. I love you, Bluebell. Stay safe. I hope you find your happiness. You'll always be in my heart."

Merigold was openly crying when she finished, snot all over her face. Her speech touched me in ways that I hadn't expected. Not for the first time, I wondered how someone so young could possess such wisdom and character.

"I have no doubts that you'll succeed, Merigold. You can do anything." I touched her cheek and wiped away some of her tears, singing a soft song of happiness. "I love you, Merigold."

Before my heart could break any further, I turned away and flew as fast as my wings could take me. But it wasn't fast enough to prevent the single teardrop from dripping out of my eye, falling to the ground with a soft plop. When it hit the grass, a golden rose immediately bloomed in its place. *Huh, I forgot that happened.*

I flew on.

"Merigold!" The voice shouting across the meadow wasn't mine, but it startled me all the same.

I stopped and turned around to observe the scene behind me. My eyes went wide when I saw Merigold's father stalking toward her. He roughly grabbed her arm when he reached her. I went on high alert. We'd hoped that he wouldn't discover I was missing until after the Bonding Ceremony. Then, Merigold could pass it off as an accident during the hustle and bustle of the Drakoni arrival. But now was too early.

"Merigold, what are you doing out here? It's late. You should be inside." He started to drag her back to the estate. It was then that he noticed the jar. "What's this?"

Merigold looked at the ground. She obviously didn't have an answer. She started to stammer, but her father's face turned red when he realized what he was looking at.

"Where is my fairy? This is the gift I gave you! You let it go, didn't you? You're weak, Merigold. You've always been weak. It was your mother's doing. She put those stupid ideas into your head. It's Drakonae females. You're not good for anything except marriage. You'll be married off to the highest bidder when you're old enough. I only hope you shape up. No one will want you like this."

My blood boiled and my vengeful side wanted to break free and attack. *This* was why I needed to stay. *This* was why Merigold needed someone. *Me.* She needed me. I would be there for her. There to defend and protect. By her side. Always.

Merigold turned her head to the ground, ashamed and unable to speak on her behalf.

"So, you think she's stupid, huh?" I muttered. I smirked, a plan forming in my mind. I zoomed down to the meadow, plucked the golden rose, and flew back to my Merigold.

I came to rest, perfectly still on her shoulder. When I sat, our hair blended together, the exact same shade of sky-blue curling together. I would have utterly disappeared if not for the fact that my skin tone was several shades lighter, my eyes were several shades darker, and my new dress that Merigold had made for me was bright gold. I smiled widely and handed the golden rose to Merigold, indicating that she should present it to her father.

Merigold looked confused but cleared her throat when I nudged her. She was a smart cookie, my Merigold.

"Father, I'm sorry. I should have told you that I've been training my fairy. Bluebell. We were just working on this. Here, it's for you." Merigold handed him the golden rose.

Her father's eyebrows rose to an almost comical height, mouth slightly gaping in surprise. He examined the rose.

"Well, Merigold. This is quite unexpected. I'm very impressed." He looked at me. "Bluebell, is it? Good name for her."

Merigold gave him a small smile. "Thank you, father."

"I expect regular status reports."

"Of course," she answered.

"Well, get to bed, then." He looked at me one more time, then walked away.

I exhaled. "Whew! That was close."

Merigold bit her lip. "Bluebell, you have to leave again! He's gone. I'll just come up with another excuse later. This is your only chance. Why did you come back?"

I smiled and patted her cheek. "I never wanted to leave, Merigold. I only left because I thought I should. Your father discovering you early gave me the perfect opportunity to come back. I was always an outcast with my family, but you've never made me feel that way. I want to stay with you, if you'll have me."

She smiled. "Of course, I want you to stay! I'd love that."

"Good. I'm glad you said that, because you're in desperate need of a fairy godmother."

"A fairy godmother?" She laughed.

I nodded. "Yes. I've recently discovered that dragon shifters are crazy, and you really need me."

"Bluebell, you do know that *I'm* a dragon shifter," she pointed out.

"Well, yes. My point stands, though. You'll need me. Trust me."

"I trust you."

"Good. That's the first step," I replied.

"What's next?"

I pursed my lips. "We'll need paper. It's a long list."

Merigold laughed. "I think I'm going to like having you as my fairy god-mother, Bluebell."

I smiled and winked. "You haven't seen anything yet, kid."

Want more Merigold and Bluebell? Check out *Skyfire: The Ascension of Merigold* (Rise of the Drakoni Book 2)! bit.ly/riseofthedrakoni

Explore the life of the Drakonae in The Evolution of Esme (A Prelude to Obsidianfire), featuring another Drakonae clan of Drakon. Read it in *The Secret Lives of Crazy Dragon Ladies* at bit.ly/DragonLadies

Our second tale is told by our Fairy of the Watering Can who flies about and gives aid to flowers and plants. Though earthbound, she dreams of other worlds and her story takes us to an alien landscape to ask the question: What if fairies were information collection devices powered by an AI? We discover the answer while looking through the eyes of a grown woman as she attempts to reconcile one fateful day from her childhood.

THE OUTCROPPING

Elizabeth Knollston

DUST ROLLED PAST THE ROVER as it came to a stop, coating the occupants of the open-concept terrain vehicle. The dry, acrid scent of the desert landscape permeated even the best enviro-suits the Corporation's engineers and suit specialists offered. The scent was oppressive and with each swallow, Katie Hunter's tongue stuck to the roof of her mouth.

Her mind toyed with the idea of a sip of water, but she ultimately decided against it. Enviro-suits were coded to their owner's bodily needs. Which meant she only had enough water for one typical day of work. And today wasn't typical.

"I should've never let you talk me into this," Jorel Freeten said with a cheeky grin. Katie glanced over at the man, who'd leaned forward, arms crossed over the steering wheel.

They'd worked together for over nine years, his nano-engineering complimenting her artificial intelligence programming work. Jorel was reliable and even-keeled, a perfect balance to her often impulsive and reckless behaviors.

"You're the one who agreed to help me with this," Katie chided.

"Right," Jorel said as he exited the rover. "Doesn't mean I should've."

With a bemused smile, Katie turned her attention to the rock formation looming in front of them.

The Outcropping, named by Geo-Survey Team Three, was composed of what they had designated Keplerite Compounds-321J, or kep-j. From the quarterly briefs all teams received, Katie knew kep-j was still being researched at a variety of Corporation labs.

"You know, these things always remind me of Sissy's French bread she insists on making," she said.

"Yeah, if she made a bunch and stuck them in a basket. Like what you see in some Old Earth footage," he added as he moved to the back of the rover and grabbed their packs. Katie snorted at Jorel's apt description.

"You good?" she asked, as Jorel tossed a pack to her.

"Yup. Systems all check out. We've got," he glanced at his left forearm and tapped on his suit's primary screen, a standard attachment to all enviro-suits, "nine hours and twenty-three minutes before the rover's due back at the dock."

"That'll just have to work," Katie said. She rolled her shoulders and tilted her head first to the right, then to the left. "This is our last chance. And I know we're close."

"Harv's pressuring you again?" Jorel asked.

Katie pursed her lips and nodded. "Won't leave it alone. Says this is the last time or else he'll report me to the Corp."

"Don't know how much of a threat that is," he replied, following after Katie.

"With my record of psych evals, it wouldn't do me any good. This is my chance to prove it. I know we're close." She stopped for a moment and raised her hand to shield her eyes from the glare of the sun as she craned her neck to look at the imposing height of The Outcropping.

To Jorel's credit, he said, "Okay."

Geo-Survey Team Three had originally tagged The Outcropping as a potential mining site, the mineral deposits within the kep-j had looked promising. As the survey had progressed, an opening into The Outcropping had been discovered. And so, the tag on The Outcropping had been updated for the xenoarch teams.

The dark and imposing entrance was nestled inside the crook of one of the many arms of rock that extended off the main portion of The Outcropping. There'd been no doubt it wasn't a naturally forming occurrence. The opening was tall and narrow, just wide enough for the average human to slip through.

"You know, you don't have anything to prove to me," Jorel said as Katie paused at the entrance.

The support and trust Jorel had in her meant more to Katie than she could ever express. And she was grateful for his continued support in the face of fallout from the rest of the team and the Corporation.

"I know. But I have something to prove to myself."

As they made their way inside The Outcropping, sensor lights, embedded in the tunnel walls flared to life, despite having been placed there over twenty years ago. Where the entrance had been narrow, the tunnel they stepped into was wide enough for them to walk side by side. The curved dome of the tunnel's ceiling provided at least a three-foot clearance above them.

Jorel brushed past her, letting her move forward at her own pace. Even with the numerous visits they'd made to The Outcropping over the past few months, each time she went inside, the memories always rushed back.

Katie closed her eyes, but the memories wouldn't remain silent. On that fateful day, she hadn't been in the main chamber when the quake had hit.

Her father had been.

After the accident on C-78, a fueling station, which had claimed the life of Katie's Mom, her father had been assigned to one of the xenoarch teams to work on unravelling The Outcropping's mysteries. All the safety protocols had been in place, as per Corporation regulations. Anyone under the age of eighteen had their suits bio-feed tied into a family member's suit. As her father had relaxed, and she'd grown comfortable with her new surroundings, she'd been allowed to explore while he worked.

THERE WAS THE OFFICIAL RECORDING of what had occurred that day. The Corporation recorded everything. Time-stamped. Location embedded. Everything cataloged and processed for future reference, and potential lawsuits. Katie had watched the vids several times, committing to memory her father's last moments.

He'd been arguing with one of his team members. Supplemental records showed an earthquake had begun to the north of The Outcropping. As the intensity increased, The Outcropping had begun to vibrate.

Katie remembered that. The slight shift of the floor, dust raining down on her. As a kid she hadn't been concerned; she'd had no understanding of what it meant. And besides, at that point, her attention had been focused on something else.

Katie opened her eyes and stepped into the main chamber, where the lights were coming to life, revealing a space far different from that of her memories.

The grand space had once had a smooth, domed ceiling, with strange, randomly spaced, squat pedestals pushed up out of the floor, and a rectangular slab centered perfectly within the circular room. Now the majority of the pedestals lay in ruins, a large portion of the ceiling having collapsed during the quake. Even the imposing slab of rock in the center now lay in pieces.

The earthquake had been devastating. Not just to The Outcropping but the entire region. More than one Corporation site had suffered damage. But only The Outcropping had suffered the loss of personnel.

"Enough memory time, we're on the clock," Jorel said. The smile he gave her was kind, despite the abrupt intrusion into her private musings.

But Jorel was right. Katie gave a sharp nod. This was her last chance to prove her memories were true, and not just the wild imaginations of a kid coping with so much loss.

"I was going over the maps we've created of the tunnel systems, and I believe we need to head back to the one where we cleared out the debris the other day."

"Then lead the way."

With a deep breath, and forcing herself to focus, Katie hefted her pack a little higher on her shoulders and led the way.

There were three other openings in the main chamber besides the one they'd just used. These three doorways lead to a maze of tunnels, all of which descended deeper into The Outcropping.

Each tunnel was like its siblings, same dimensions, same smooth walls. Katie didn't need her suit's ability to pull up an HDR-map to know where she needed to go.

While her father had worked, Katie had wandered the tunnels, memorizing them. The stories her Mom had read to her as a child had filled The Outcropping, until it was bursting with tales of lost kingdoms, crashing waves against jagged cliffs, legendary races of Old Earth able to wield magic, strange creatures who hoarded gold, and the large, terrible fire-breathing beasts who stalked the lands.

One of the reasons no one had believed her.

They passed the debris field they'd cleared, and Katie's chest tightened. Not out of fear, but excitement. She knew this was the right way. The tunnel she needed to prove she wasn't crazy.

Katie reached out, and let her hand run along the tunnel's wall. "I know most teenagers don't have their heads full of Old Earth myths and legends. And it was probably a coping mechanism after Mom died, I'll admit that. But what I've truly believed," Katie paused. She hadn't given voice to this part of her, but she needed to today. "What I know in my heart, is that it was all meant to be. Those stories Mom told me, the love of mysteries and puzzles from my Dad, that I had to have those to believe what I saw, what I know happened was real."

She didn't need Jorel to respond, and he didn't. Just being able to say the words out loud lifted a weight she'd been carrying for so long.

As they made their way deeper inside The Outcropping, Katie let herself reminisce, telling Jorel a few of her favorite bedtime stories, and then eventually drifted off into silence.

"End of the line," Jorel broke through the quiet.

Katie turned and beamed at him. "No, now we're just at the beginning."

She knelt down and motioned for Jorel to join her. With a touch, she brought up her suit's lights at her shoulders and wrists, aiming their illumination towards the lower half of the walls of the tunnel.

"The xenoteams did make note of the random glyphs found within the tunnels, but most of their research was concentrated up in the main chamber. Especially considering how hard the Corporation was pushing for mining, they felt that was their first priority to document."

"I saw some the other day we were here," Jorel commented. He leaned forward and brushed his hand over some of the strange glyphs.

"The xenoarchs should have put more effort into them," Katie murmured. "Tell me what you feel."

Jorel switched positions, so he was kneeling in front of the alien markings. He ran his hand back over the glyphs several times before leaning away and shaking his head. Katie smiled and took his hand in hers.

She pushed his fingers against the glyphs, tracing every mark. Katie watched Jorel's face, waiting for his "ah-ha" expression; raised eyebrows, eyes wide, and a grin which always followed.

"Holy shit," Jorel said.

"I know, right?"

"You don't read the glyphs, you have to feel them, don't you?" he said in building excitement. "Just like, damn, what was it? That Old Earth method of reading for the blind."

"Braille, but instead of raised bumps, here they're indented. Pretty clever right?"

"You bet it is. Makes me wonder if the aliens who built this had limited vision, or why a tactile way of communicating was important."

"I know, so many possibilities," Katie added.

Jorel shook his head, "What a waste no one figured this out before."

"From what I've read, there were a few teams who came back after the quake and did some preliminary research, but by the time the Corp declared the area safe, its focus had shifted to other sectors of the planet. So those teams only had limited resources and time. Everything was tagged and flagged for follow-up."

"But no one ever did," Jorel finished for her.

"Nope, and this isn't even the best part."

Everything was beginning to feel like she'd been here only the day before. Her mind filled with wild stories, and her focus on solving a puzzle.

There were five different glyphs. Through hours of experimentation, Katie had figured out they had to be touched in a specific sequence.

The first was a cluster of three small indented dots. The second was a single, vertical line. The third, was a series of vertical lines, cut through their centers by a horizontal line of indented dots. The fourth glyph was another cluster of three dots but enclosed within an oval. The fifth glyph, her favorite, was a vertical line, much deeper than the others, and when one really pressed their fingers against it, they could feel another series of dots, cut much deeper than the line.

Katie lifted her fingers from the last glyph and Jorel took a sharp breath in. "Well, I'll be damned."

Each glyph became illuminated by a soft, blue light emanating from somewhere behind it. In less than a minute, the glow was strong enough to light the floor of the tunnel.

Leaving Jorel in stunned silence, Katie stood and moved just a few feet away and pressed an index finger into one single, solitary divot in the wall.

As she moved back, the same hue of blue appeared. This light was stronger than the others and lit up the end of the tunnel.

"Look," Katie pointed with a huge grin plastered on her face.

What had once been the end of the tunnel, was now an entrance to another chamber.

Jorel whistled and ran his hand through his hair. "I've always believed you, I swear I have. But to see this in person, it's something else."

Katie's grin only grew. "Pretty mind-blowing, huh?"

"Yeah," was Jorel's only response, as he stared, open-mouthed at the newly revealed room.

Katie stepped inside and looked around. It was just as she remembered. Another weight was lifted from her mind, as she'd feared what it would have meant if this room had suffered damage at some point. But it hadn't.

The room was round, just like the main chamber, only smaller, more intimate in size. There were no pedestals or central slab. Instead, from the rock, different sets of shelves had been created. Each shelf was thick and had cylindrical protrusions coming out from the bottom. Glyphs had been carved in-between the sets of shelving and on the edges of each shelf.

"Some sort of lab? Or storage space?" Jorel asked as he stepped into the room. He took off his pack, laid it next to the doorway, and began to look around.

"I mean those ideas make sense," Katie said. "But this is the room. This is where they came from."

"Oh, okay, so more assembly or workshop type space then," Jorel said. He pointed to a shelf and the odd protrusions underneath it. "Containers?"

"Yup. Don't know exactly-" Katie began to say. "Wait, don't do-" But her admonishment was too late.

Jorel had reached out, trying to see what was in one of the containers. But instead of pulling something out, he yelped in pain and jumped back.

"Sorry, you okay?" Katie asked. "I should have said something right away."

Jorel shook his hand, wincing as his fingers still smarted. "No, it's alright. Should have known better anyway."

"It'll take a bit for the pain to go away," Katie added. She remembered doing the same thing when she was a kid.

"Some type of shielding then. Either a precious resource or a dangerous resource?" Jorel mumbled.

"Whatever it is, whatever all this is, it's way beyond our tech level," Katie commented.

"Gee, no kidding," Jorel snorted. "So, you ready, then?"

Katie's stomach turned sour. Where she'd felt excitement only a few moments before, now she was beginning to feel a growing sense of dread. She pressed her hands against her thighs, the slick material of the suit something familiar.

"Sure," she finally said.

Jorel glanced at her and his expression softened. "Hey, it's okay." He glanced at his suit's readout. "We've still got plenty of time. Everything has been just like you described, this isn't going to be any different."

Katie frowned. "Tell that to all the docs who kept saying I was hallucinating, and building it all from comforting memories to help me through a difficult time." Her dread began to mix with long-held frustration and anger. "I told them everything, in detail. Why would I make that stuff up? I begged them to come back, to prove to them what I saw. What happened to me that day."

"It's too bad your video feed was damaged," Jorel added, trying to help.

Katie threw him a look of disgust. "I know, but it was too corrupted for even their best techs to recover it."

Dread, anger, frustration churned inside of her, hardening to a thick blanket of resolve. Pulling her shoulders back, Katie moved to stand next to a cluster of glyphs. "After I discovered the room, I figured the same idea would work in here. Find a sequence of glyphs to make something happen. It was just another puzzle. I tried different combinations for days with no luck."

Katie reached out, her handing hovering above one of the glyphs. "I was drawn to this set, and so this is where I focused my attention."

As her fingertips brushed the first glyph, her suit's notification alarm sounded, followed by Jorel's.

"I don't believe it," Jorel groaned. "We've got seismic activity just south of us."

"What?" Katie asked in alarm, bringing up the alert.

"I don't think it's going to be an issue though," Jorel added, scrolling through the data. "Looks like one of the smaller ones, probably a controlled test as the teams work on moving forward in the next phase for the colony."

"You sure?" Katie asked, feeling her stomach tighten.

"Yup," Jorel said as he double-checked the figures. "We're fine." He lowered his arm and saw the panicked look on Katie's face. "Hey, it's okay. Just breathe... do the count of four thing."

The quakes had lessened over time as the Corporation worked on stabilizing the planet and making it suitable for a new colony. But no matter how much therapy or education she did over the quakes, the threat of one always threw her mind into a panic.

"Why don't you sit for a minute," Jorel said. "Clear your thoughts." She felt him pick up her wrist and check her suits bio-feed. "Looks like we can administer some meds to help, you want to?"

Katie hated the idea. She hated having to rely on medication to help at times. But the anxiousness which had already been gnawing on her, combined with the quake warning was too much. She couldn't waste her last chance to prove she'd been right.

She nodded and gave him the codes. There was a slight pinch just below her collar bone, and within a few seconds, she could feel her body beginning to relax.

"Thanks."

"No problem, that's what friends are for," Jorel said and bent forward to place a gentle kiss on her forehead. He moved back over to where he'd lain his pack down and bent over to pick it up. "I've got some extra ration bars in here somewhere."

Their suit's alerts went off again, this time much louder. More urgent.

But it was too late.

The room began to shake, dust rained down all around them. There was a crack, like the sizzle of lighting spread against a thunderous sky.

"We've got to go!" Jorel shouted. As he reached towards her, the ceiling split open and large chunks of rock fell around them.

"Jorel!" Katie screamed as the force of a large portion of the roof crashing down in front of her, flung her back up against the wall. Her head slammed into the rock, and while the suit did what it could, it wasn't enough to prevent Katie from slipping into darkness.

AS KATIE GRADUALLY CAME BACK to consciousness, a knot of pain was centered in her lower back, with tendrils extending out into the rest of her body. Dust floated in the air, drying her throat and forcing a series of coughs. The pain intensified with each cough until the world went black once more.

AS SHE AWOKE FOR THE second time, the dust had settled. The pain was still present, and Katie checked her bio-feed. Despite slamming into the wall, she'd been lucky. She'd hurt like hell, and be a walking bruise, but no broken bones.

After any medical emergency, the enviro-suits automatic coding was to prompt for emergency treatment. Katie checked what had been administered, and punched in her code for another dose of pain meds. As she struggled to stand, she made the snap decision to also key in a dose of stimulants. As the drugs began to work, and the pain eased, she tried to take stock of the situation. But it was difficult to separate the memories from reality.

For a moment, Katie thought she was in the main chamber, looking at the pile of debris that had crushed her father. She blinked and struggled to regain control as the room spun. Stumbling, she reached out and leaned against the wall. Her chest began to tighten, and her skin tingled.

"Dad?" she whimpered. No, she shook her head. That wasn't right. It wasn't her father. "Hello?" she called out.

Silence answered her.

What was she missing? Katie tried to take a deep breath, but couldn't. Her chest was tight, and her stomach threatened to empty itself. Just breath, she berated herself. Just try to breathe. Deep breath in. Hold. Let it out. Hold.

Reciting those words helped loosen the block in her mind. Her head snapped up and Katie shouted, "Jorel!"

She clawed at her suit's screen, fumbling in her panic to bring up the HDR-map of The Outcropping. "Show me the location of Jorel Freeten. Give me all bio-feed info." The screen went to the Corporation's logo as the system worked. "No, dammit. Come on, where is he?"

Panic crept in as each second ticked by until the screen blinked, the HDR-map spreading out before her. Two green dots appeared, one with her ID code and one with Jorel's.

He was on the other side of the debris blocking the entrance to the room. Katie scrolled through the bio-feed and felt her stomach tighten. A fractured tibia in the left leg. Two broken ribs. Internal bleeding. First aid had been given, but he needed far more than what the suit could offer.

Katie squeezed her eyes shut, trying to block out the panic. The images she'd seen of her father being crushed to death. Her knees buckled, and she cried out in pain as she collapsed. She couldn't go through it again. Katie didn't know if she could survive losing another person she loved. Not like this. Not here.

Her suit chimed, sending a warning her blood pressure was dangerously high. Another chime and the suit advised another dose of meds. It would still be within acceptable levels. Without thinking, Katie accepted.

Warmth flooded her body, and Katie knew she had to keep it together. Jorel was counting on her. He'd followed her on this fool's errand. She wasn't going to be responsible for his death.

Once more, she struggled to her feet and truly began to look around the room. A large portion of the ceiling had collapsed, blocking the entrance. But the majority of the room was intact. A few of the shelves appeared to have cracks in them, but nothing that should cause her any immediate danger.

The problem was getting to Jorel, and then how to get him to the rover without causing him to go critical. Their suits would have alerted their team's central network of the trauma and a rescue unit would be sent.

But it would be a race against time. Would the rescue team be able to get here in time to help Jorel? Or could Katie get him out, and to help sooner? The team would have to follow safety protocols, of ensuring the area was safe, and there was no telling how much debris would be in their way.

That thought settled, and Katie felt her body tighten with fear. If there was debris in other places, it'd be a huge roadblock for her too. She wasn't an engineer, just an AI specialist. She didn't have the skills or knowledge needed to figure out these problems. Let alone the equipment.

Even though she could reprogram the suits to do whatever she wanted, they couldn't give her superhuman strength to move the debris. Last time, they'd brought equipment with them to help with that. And as she eyed the pile of rocks, she wasn't sure she even wanted to attempt to move it. Moving one rock would affect the position of the others. Which ones would be safe to remove first? What if she made it worse and the rocks collapsed further inside the room or, even worse, onto Jorel?

Desperate for a solution, Katie went ahead and reprogrammed a few of the suit's systems. She swung her arm out, pointed at the pile of rubble. The suit scanned, and in a few minutes provided a few different options. But none of them were great, and the suit projected further collapse each time.

"Shit," Katie said. "Update. Jorel's vitals," she commanded. The readout showed he was stable and still unconscious. At least that was something, she thought.

Looking through the options on moving the debris, Katie finally settled on one. She had to try something. Within moving the first couple of rocks, her back was screaming at her, and she tried just rolling them. The pain was only intensified. Sweat coated her hair, neck, and underneath the suit.

Having to stop, Katie let herself slide down the wall. Without thinking, she let her head rest against the cool stone and closed her eyes.

Katie jerked awake. She looked at her suit's screen. "You stupid fool." She'd fallen asleep for over an hour. Jorel's vitals had changed. His blood pressure had dropped and his temperature was going up. "I should've never come back here," she yelled at herself. "Just to prove some stupid story."

And then it struck her. The whole damn reason she'd brought Jorel here. The doctors had never believed her, not just telling her she'd been hallucinating, but that there was no way she'd been where she'd said she was. The pile of debris she and Jorel had been forced to move to get here, had been only one of several which had clogged the tunnels after the quake. How could a kid have made it through all of that?

She pulled herself up and knew what she had to do. The pain had spread to her hips and shoulders, made her shuffle to the cluster of glyphs she'd always been drawn to. Her hand trembled as she reached out, and hovered just above the first glyph.

She was afraid. What if she had hallucinated it all? Then there wasn't anything she could do but wait for help. And she felt certain Jorel wouldn't be able to hold on until then. But if it was true, then it was their way out of The Outcropping.

It had to be true.

With more force than what was necessary, Katie ran her fingers over the first glyph. The second, the third, and the fourth. This time as her finger finished a glyph, brilliant yellow light illuminated them, and a corresponding glyph on the shelves. The light extended from the glyph of the edge of the shelf to wrap around each corresponding container. The vivid lights bled into the wall, converging on each other into a fat line of light both down towards the floor and up to the ceiling. Together the lines of light traveled to the center of the room.

Without thinking, Katie held her breath as she watched the two points of light extend out towards the other and meet in the middle as if somehow contained in an invisible tube.

There was a brilliant flash of light, followed by three more, and suspended inside the tube of light was the whole reason she'd come back. Her hallucinations had been real after all.

It was her fairy.

Just as she'd pictured all those years ago when her Mom had read to her at bedtime. It had a humanoid shape, with two translucent wings attached just below each shoulder blade. The head had the appearance of a tear-drop, and long pointed ears, with the tips dipping down towards its back.

There was one last flash of light, so bright Katie had to throw up her arm to shield her eyes. When she could turn back to look, the light was gone and the fairy hovered just a few feet away from her.

Katie felt like screaming, laughing, and crying all at once. She'd been right this whole time. Through their stubborn ignorance and dismissal of a kid, they'd missed something so important, that even Katie had a hard time comprehending.

Startled out of her awe, her suit chimed. She wiped at her tears and glanced at the screen. Fear clawed at her as she stared at the error message.

Waiting for a rescue team wasn't a good option, it was a last resort considering how Jorel was in such bad shape. But it had been an option.

The error message took even that sliver of hope away. The suits had done as programmed and attempted to send the SOS message. But each attempt, a cycle of four tries within each hour, had failed. There was no rescue coming, they'd never received the SOS. They were too far underground, and the kep-j was somehow interfering with their suits ability to communicate past a few hundred yards.

If Jorel was going to make it through this, then Katie had to figure it out. She lifted her eyes and stared at the fairy. No one was coming. All she had was herself, her suit, and the fairy. And she wasn't going to let Jorel die.

When she was a kid, the fairy had gotten her safely back to the main chamber. Katie knew that without a doubt. What she didn't know, was how it'd happened. She studied the fairy, noting it flapped its wings every few seconds. If she took a step in any direction, the fairy moved as well, but always maintained at least a two-foot distance between them. If Katie turned her back to it, the fairy would move, so it would once again be within her line of sight.

There were a thousand questions crowding Katie's mind. And if there was time and the proper equipment, she'd indulge herself. But right now, the only thing that mattered was figuring out how to get the fairy to help her and Jorel.

"What are you?" Katie asked. It was an open-ended question, but she needed to start somewhere. The wings rippled and appeared to shine for a brief moment. But that was its only response.

Katie frowned. "Who are you?" Another brief ripple of light within the wings.

"Katie?"

For a brief moment, Katie thought the fairy had said her name, but as the voice called again, she gave herself a shake and tapped the comms on her suit.

"Jorel? Don't try to move. You've been badly injured." She took a breath, and when there wasn't a response, "Jorel? Are you still there? Come in."

"I'm...I think I'm alright. I guess." He coughed, and Katie cringed at the wet sound within it. "My suit says my vitals aren't great. I can't move my leg though."

"It's okay. Don't try to move anything. Just stay there and I'm coming to you. I'll get you out, and then we'll go get help." Katie desperately tried to believe what she was saying.

"Where are you? Injuries?"

"I'm okay. Just some bumps and bruises are all. Just working on a way to get us out of here."

There was another long stretch of silence. Katie tried calling Jorel a few more times, and when she didn't receive an answer, she checked his bio-feed. He'd slipped into unconsciousness again. And his vitals were still deteriorating.

For a brief moment, she considered overriding his system and forcing it to dose him again. But if she did that, she might regret it later. The amount of emergency medication a suit carried was limited. Jorel could use a dose of meds now, but what if he became critical and she'd depleted the suits store of medication?

She stopped and decided to wait.

"Damn," Katie cursed. She glared at the fairy, at the wall of debris blocking her exit, and then began to pace. As she moved, she began to talk through the situation, "I can't move the stupid rocks because I could injury myself, Jorel, or make the whole situation worse. I don't want to hijack his system yet; I've got to save that for the last resort. There's no equipment to allow me to boost the signal. Shit."

Katie stopped and had to sit, her pain steadily increasing. She had very little to work with. And she was tired. She was scared. And her back and hips were screaming at her.

"Equipment."

Katie stiffened. "Jorel?" But she checked his bio-feed. There'd been no change.

"Signal. System. Shit."

Her eyes moved to the fairy, and she felt her stomach tighten in fear and anticipation.

"Boost signal. No equipment."

Pain momentarily forgotten; Katie got to her feet. "What did you just say?"

"What did...you just...say," it said in its soft, mechanical voice.

Katie leaned closer, the hairs on the back of her neck standing up. "How are you able to speak Standard?"

The fairy again repeated Katie's words, and then an incoherent jumble of things Katie had already said.

Katie rocked back on her heels as she listened to it. "I don't know why I didn't think of that. Of course, you'd have some sort of intelligence, some equivalent of artificial intelligence programming. You're just learning the parameters of the system."

Again, the fairy repeated her words, and then again in a mixed-up jumble.

"Okay, alright. We can do this," Katie said. And then she began to talk. She worked through several snippets of her favorite bedtime stories, bits and pieces from technical manuals, and threw in some random lyrics for kicks. Pausing each time to let the fairy repeat her words, until finally instead of spitting out a mixed-up version, it began to put words together in new ways. In phrases and then sentences she hadn't said.

"Language acquisition complete." The fairy said. "Field survey parameters."

"What?" Katie frowned. While communication had been established, she knew there was still a wide gulf between them, preventing true understanding. Its translation of Standard was dependent upon its alien cultural references, not human ones.

Katie shook herself, none of it mattered. Right now, she only had one priority. She had to get to Jorel. Then the xenoarch teams could sort everything out later.

"This debris," she moved over to the obstacle, "needs to be removed. But carefully, Jorel is on the other side, and he's already injured."

The fairy had turned and watched her. But nothing else.

Crap, she thought. What if it needs a specific set of codes? Or specific words to make it do something? If only I could remember exactly what I did when I was a kid, she thought as she began to grow angry with herself.

Katie let out a frustrated sigh and rolled her neck to try to work out some of the tension she was feeling. But as she did, her eyes caught on something in the ceiling. Katie froze. Whatever it was, was gone. No, wait. She moved her head again, and there it was. As she moved back and forth, whatever was in the ceiling would appear and then disappear.

"What is that?" she mumbled.

She moved to stand directly underneath it and craned her neck to try to get a better look. When that didn't work, she lifted her left arm, and let her suit scan the area. The majority of the information the suit provided was beyond her. And she suspected it would be for most.

What she was seeing was unlike anything she'd ever come across before. The suit did detect some kind of large, tube-like structure within the ceiling, but whatever the material, the suit couldn't identify it. What was more, it wasn't the only one. The suit picked up on an intricate network of the stuff, running throughout the entire ceiling. She figured the kep-j in the rock had hidden this gold mine of information from all the scans she and other teams had done before.

"Duh, Katie. It makes sense. Whatever those things are, they must channel the light. I just wonder if it's all throughout The Outcropping." She moved over to a part of the wall and laid her hand on it. "But more importantly, where does it go?" She asked as she began to think of a plan.

"The central nervous system of the ungvota leads to the heart of the oprotva egifr."

The fairy startled Katie, and she jumped. "Say that again?"

It did.

And then she had it repeat it once more. She tried for a translation or approximation for the words which didn't make sense. But the fairy could give neither.

"Okay, okay," she rubbed her eyes and sighed. "It doesn't matter. They're probably proper names for something." She moved underneath the exposed tubing. "Where does that go?"

The fairy repeated the same statement.

Katie scowled. "No, I mean, where does this," she sighed, "central nervous system go from this room?" And then without thinking she added, "Show me."

The fairy didn't verbally respond. Instead, it flew up to the exposed tubing, pointing at it as it moved towards the blocked doorway. And then it moved through the rock.

"Holy shit, wait, no comeback!" Katie cried out.

And then pleaded.

And then she felt fear clouding everything else out. No matter what she said, or yelled, the fairy didn't return.

Then as if a dam had burst, anger erupted inside of her. How could she have been so careless? She'd just lost her chance at helping Jorel. Why couldn't she have remembered what she'd done when she was a kid?

Tears began to flow freely, and Katie collapsed. Her energy was spent. Her mind was numb with fear and anger. She cried until she felt as if she was going to throw up. The pain was becoming overwhelming, and all she wanted to do was curl up into a ball and close her eyes. Maybe it was all a dream, another hallucination and if she just slept for a bit, she'd wake and everything would be back to normal.

Katie let her body go slack, and she lay on the cold, hard floor. She closed her eyes, and let the exhaustion, pain, fear, and anger wash over her. As she lay there, her mind began to drift and unwind, and she moved in and out of memories. And then it hit her.

The solution was so simple.

Struggling to just sit, Katie knew she needed another dose of meds. She keyed in her code and then had to use the override function to get the last dose her suit had.

It only took a few moments for the pain to lessen, and Katie got to her feet and with a fierce determination, moved over to her cluster of glyphs. In a matter of minutes, she turned and watched a new fairy come to life.

With a rueful smile, she watched this new fairy. An identical match. Its movements the same, tracking her and maintaining a two feet distance.

Alright, she thought, here we go. And she began to recite everything she'd said before, and more until at last this fairy spoke.

"Language acquisition complete. Field survey parameters."

The idea of using the tubing as a way to escape the room was still valid. She just needed to choose her words carefully. There was a lot of room for error.

First things first. "Do not leave my side."

"Accepted."

Katie breathed a sigh of relief. She had to believe that meant it at least understood that command.

She studied the tubing, and then the data her suit had provided. It was limited, but she felt certain the tubing must extend out into the tunnel where Jorel was. But she wanted to know for certain before attempting anything.

"Can you show me a map or a representative form such as this," she motioned to the HDR-map the suit had created, "to show me where that tubing goes."

Katie held her breath. If this didn't work, she had no idea how many more fairies she could make. Plus, time was against her.

The fairy moved closer to the HDR-map, hovered in front of it for a few seconds, and then there was a brilliant flash of light. When the spots were gone from her vision, Katie saw the fairy had moved towards a section of the wall. For a second, she panicked and thought this fairy was going to leave her too.

It didn't, to her relief and shock. The fairy touched the wall, and the wall disappeared. Just as the doorway to this room had been revealed. Cautiously, Katie took a few steps towards the newly revealed door. What lay beyond it was darkness.

She turned on the rest of the lights on her suit, and from what she could make out, it looked like the fairy was showing her another kind of tunnel. But this one was at least triple the width of the others, and as Katie took a few more steps forward, her suit's lights revealed various shapes and sizes of rock jutting out of the walls on either side.

Katie was about ready to step into the darkness when she realized the obvious. If the fairy could somehow remove a part of the rock, then why couldn't it do the same to the debris?

"Fairy," she started, "do not leave me, but touch the debris here," she moved to indicate the area, "and remove it just as you removed that wall."

"There is no doorway," the fairy said.

Katie huffed in frustration. "Yes, of course, there is! It's just blocked by the part of the ceiling that collapsed. Touch it and remove it."

"There is no doorway," the fairy repeated.

"It's right here," Katie almost shouted. She moved as close as she could, a few of the smaller rocks tumbling out of her way. "Here, here's the doorway into the tunnel. Jorel is on the other side. Remove these rocks," she slapped them, "so I can get to Jorel!"

"There is no doorway," the fairy said yet again.

This time Katie screamed. "But there is, it's right-" And then she stopped. Her face flushed with embarrassment. A doorway. The fairy needed a doorway. The rocks were from the ceiling, not a part of the wall or what had been the entrance.

"Does the subject wish to proceed?" the fairy asked.

Katie's tear-stained face looked up and with a defeated look she nodded. "Yes, I do."

She climbed off the rocks and took a step into the corridor. "Lights?" she quietly asked.

The fairy floated to the inside of the doorway from the corridor side and touched something. Gentle, blue light began to fill the corridor. Katie glanced to look at what the fairy had touched. It was another glyph, one she felt she recognized but hadn't used before.

The fairy moved down the corridor and then turned. "Follow."

Katie didn't need to be told twice. She had to get to Jorel. She glanced at his bio-feed. His blood pressure was holding steady, but his temperature was climbing. She didn't need a medical degree to know time was running out.

Even as her energy was waning, Katie couldn't help but wonder what each of the giant slabs of rock was as the fairy passed them by. All had glyphs carved into them; on the tops, sides, and she noted even a few carved into the floor. What had the alien race who'd created such a place even looked like? Was it something like the creation which was leading her? But why would it look like a fairy from the myths and legends of Old Earth? Did that mean the fairies or who had ever created them had at some point been on Earth? The implications were far too much for her to consider.

The fairy abruptly stopped and turned to its right. This slab of rock slanted down from the ceiling, and then changed angles and jutted out into the corridor. When Katie was standing in front of it, the fairy touched a series of glyphs on the edge of the slab. Katie tried to keep track of which glyphs and in what order the fairy touched them, but there were so many, and she was so tired, she lost track.

When it finished, Katie had a hard time believing what she was seeing. The rocky surface was transformed. And for the first time, the thought crossed Katie's mind, what if the kep-j found within The Outcropping was a part of this alien technology?

As the surface became more translucent, it looked as if the inside was a jumbled mess of interconnecting thinly spun tubes. As she leaned forward to take a closer look, the surface changed and for a split-second, she feared she'd inadvertently triggered something. As she jerked backward, the surface again changed, this time with the appearance of a dull, metallic covering. But then sections of it began to glow.

Yellows, blues, and purples danced before her eyes. As if she was watching a pond of fish dart back and forth beneath a frozen covering of ice. She knew it was indeed some type of map. But without a frame of reference or an understanding of the entire layout of The Outcropping, this idea was proving to be useless.

"I need a way to get to Jorel," she growled.

In her haze of despair, it took her a minute to realize the fairy had begun to move deeper within the corridor.

"No, stop, wait!"

But the fairy did no such thing.

"Dammit," Katie muttered and moved as quickly as her body would let her. She tried again to get the fairy to stop, but it wouldn't. Feeling out of control and with nothing left to lose, Katie just surrendered and followed it.

They passed several intersections, but it wasn't until the fourth one that the fairy turned left. Katie gave a nervous glance at her suit's screen. She would soon be out of range to communicate with Jorel's suit. Whatever the fairy thought it was supposed to do, Katie hoped it would happen quickly.

The tunnel they turned into began to widen, and Katie could sense they were ascending now. The idea of moving up, lifted her spirits, and thought maybe the fairy knew a different way out of The Outcropping. Katie could at least then double back the way she and Jorel had entered and get to him.

But as soon as she began to feel hopeful, it was gone.

The fairy stopped. It wasn't from indecision, or that it appeared there was something useful in the area. It had come to a block in the corridor. Something that was the result of one of the quakes.

"Is there a way around this? To wherever you were taking me?" Katie asked.

The fairy turned to face her. "No."

The simplicity of the response was like a slap to her face. Frustration and fear soured to disgust. "What good are you then?"

"Field survey parameters."

"That doesn't mean anything to me," Katie snapped.

She was out of options. She gritted her teeth. That wasn't quite true. She could work on removing the rocks and hope she could get to Jorel. And if she didn't injure herself further, she'd crawl through whatever opening she could make and then assess the situation from there. Provided she didn't collapse more of the ceiling on herself or cave it in onto Jorel. Decision made, Katie ignored the fairy, turned, and retraced her steps.

By the time she made it back to what she'd dubbed as the fairy room, her whole body felt weak. There was no way she was going to be able to move anything without giving her body a rest.

Katie made it to where she'd left her pack, Jorel's having been lost under the crush of rock. Most of what had been inside having been crushed when she'd been thrown up against the wall. But she dug out the crumbled remnants of the ration bars in her pack, and let herself drink what was left of her water.

As she ate the ration bar crumbs, she eyed the fairy which had followed her. A part of her was still impressed, but she felt mostly resentment towards it, its lack of being able to help. She let her thoughts begin to dip towards the darker fears. Jorel was going to die here, and it was her fault. She was going to die here.

Just like her father. But her death would be far more painful. She'd starve to death. Slow and painful. Perhaps that was fitting considering she'd led Jorel to his death.

If she did, by some miracle, make it out alive, she'd be in for serious disciplinary action. Even with the discovery, she'd made. The Corporation would have to make an example out of her. She'd have wasted resources on a rescue mission, and more than likely cost them the life of a good employee.

Katie laid down, exhaustion washing over her. The food and the water hadn't helped. Instead, her stomach felt tight, and she was beginning to shiver. Hand trembling, she tried to key in the codes for another dose of meds, only to be reminded she'd already used all her suit had to offer.

She glanced up, the fairy still there, hovering just a few feet away from her. Ever watching. Always observing.

Curling her body uptight, Katie told herself she'd just rest for a few minutes, and then she'd work on trying to remove the rocks. But spent and worn both physically and mentally, Katie drifted off to sleep.

LAUGHTER CHASED HER, BOUNCING OFF the smooth surface of the tunnels. Katie ran up and down, playing hide-and-seek with her new friend. As she darted around the corner of one of the tunnel junctions, Katie skidded to a stop.

Fear darted through her as the floor began to tremble. And then it was gone and so was her fear. Katie laughed and chased after her friend.

"Found you," a grin split her face as she rounded another turn, and saw her friend's light spilling throughout the tunnel.

But then the floor did more than tremble, it shook. Violently. Katie lost her footing and was thrown against the wall. She cried, pain blossoming in her shoulder. "Dad? Dad, what's going on?" she yelled into her suit's comm system.

But his reply never came. Instead, dust began to coat her hair, skin, and suit. And then bits of rock fell as if she was standing in the middle of a hail storm. Katie turned to run, but a side of the wall gave out, collapsing into the tunnel. There was a deafening crack and the floor split. Katie tumbled back, trying to scramble out of the way of the widening crack.

"Dad, Dad please! Help me!" she screamed over and over.

The only reply was the light of her new friend. It spread across her, the light was both warm and calming. Her friend had reached down and extended a hand, and not knowing what to do, Katie had reached out and taken it.

KATIE WOKE WITH A START, and she knew. How she'd made it back to the main chamber all those years ago. The fairy had saved her.

It'd saved her by doing what she'd watched the first fairy do, only a while ago. The fairy had actually taken her through the rock walls. Katie cursed and mentally kicked herself. Why hadn't she been able to realize this before? Why hadn't she been able to remember when she watched the fairy do it?

Because she thought. I'm tired. I'm scared. And I've had so many years of doctors telling me what I knew was possible, wasn't. But as a kid, there'd never been any questioning as to what was possible. She'd reached out in a time of need. And the fairy had somehow known what she needed.

Katie cried out in pain as she forced herself to stand. She took her pack with her, gingerly swinging it up on a shoulder.

The fairy was still there.

Waiting.

Katie stepped forward and this time knew there was no need for words or commands. She simply needed help.

She reached out her hand.

And she waited. She believed. Anything was possible. She needed help. She needed to get to Jorel. Over and over, she thought those things.

The fairy moved, and it extended its hand and touched hers.

The light of the fairy washed over her, just as she remembered it. Warm and calming. The light grew until Katie had to close her eyes. Her skin began to tingle as if she was touching some kind of electrical current.

She pushed all other thoughts out of her mind. Simply focused on her need. On getting to Jorel.

As soon as it had started, it was over. The warmth faded, and she opened her eyes. Not trying to think about what just happened, she dropped to Jorel's side. She grabbed his arm and tapped at his screen. His vitals were declining, but she overrode his system and forced the suit to give the last doses of meds it had left.

Holding her breath, she waited and watched. Slowly, but gradually his bio-feed began to show Jorel was stabilizing. Katie cradled his arm and cried. He was still in bad shape, but she still had a chance to get him the help he needed. Now she just had to get him out of The Outcropping. And once outside of the kep-j rock, she desperately hoped she'd be able to get a signal out.

Jorel stirred, and Katie brushed his hair off his forehead. "Hey, there. It's going to be okay. We'll get you out of here. And everything will be fine, okay?"

"Katie?" his voice was rough.

"Shh, don't try to talk. Just rest. I'll get you help."

She watched as he tried to focus on her, and then his eyes darted to the side. "Is that–?"

Katie nodded. "Yup."

"I knew you weren't crazy," Jorel smiled. Then his face contorted in pain and was racked by a fit of coughing.

"Hey, no talking I said." Katie tried to soothe him. "Once you're all patched up, I'll tell you all about it."

Jorel nodded and closed his eyes.

Face streaked with tears, she looked up at the fairy. She knew without a doubt that everything was going to be okay. She gripped one of Jorel's hands with her own, and then stretched her other hand out to the fairy.

The fairy floated down and touched Katie's offered hand.

Katie smiled. She didn't think about anything that could go wrong or the impossibilities of it all.

She pictured the rover, the hot sun of the desert beating down upon them. She envisioned Jorel safely aboard the rover, strapped in and secure as she headed out to meet the rescue teams.

Katie believed in the impossible as light flooded the tunnel, wrapping itself around them.

Our Tell-It-Like-It-Is Fairy has written a story about a character who has lost his way. He doesn't have anyone to tell him like it is—and it's doubtful he would listen if he did. But an unexpected encounter in the middle of a storm has the potential to set him on a new path. If only he is brave enough to take it.

A PLACE TO START

Ember Fane

THE SCENT OF WARM STONE mingled with the fresh rainfall. As the large drops plopped into puddles, and then sank into the ground, the rich aroma of wet earth lifted into the saturated air, the scent almost over-powering in its thickness.

Ignoring the wondrous layers of the world's natural perfumes which surrounded him, Zephyrus Shimmerbreeze huddled in the cleft of a boulder that rose smoothly out of the meadow grasses beyond the southernmost suburb of the Enchanted City. The gray and brown striated stone was nearly as large as a pony. Time had worn it smooth but had also cracked it. That crack had become a cleft, narrow at the top, wide at the base, and traveling deep into the rock. Zeph had crawled into this natural shelter until he could go no farther.

The *sprityan* sat with his knees drawn up, his head resting on the yellow linen leggings that covered them. His amber and sky-blue wings drooped, hanging forwards along his sides like a cape. Hugging his arms tighter around his lower legs, he sighed.

It was another fine mess in which he found himself. Hungover—again. Hiding from law enforcement—again. Showing off for a set of fine legs and causing chaos—again. Looking to place the blame anywhere but on his own four and a half inch wide shoulders.

He could just hear his father's angry words. See his mother's tightly pressed lips as she turned away. Feel the cold stare of his grandmother's gaze. Know that his siblings would barely bat an eyelash as they went about their lives. Zeph, being Zeph, they would think.

The need to run gnawed away in the pit of his stomach, an all too familiar ache. It battled with the pang of despair in his heart.

To where would he go? Home to the Celestial Spires was out of the question. Now, he'd ruined any opportunity to remain in the Enchanted City or its environs. Neither the City of Ash nor the Sunken Kingdom appealed to him, less so the Wastelands where ancient banners long decayed to strands of thread whipped about in the wind that sang of death.

With a groan, Zeph leaned his head back against the rock and wished himself never hatched.

A roar of thunder followed a particularly loud and bright crack of lightning. Right behind it, a high-pitched squeal as a young *pix* ran into the cleft's shelter. Three or four inches tall, the pix was in his later childhood. His long tunic was woven from dockroot and worn over leggings torn off at mid-thigh. His clothing was soaked. An acorn shell served as a head covering—though it was useless for keeping the rain off the pix's delicate features.

The little pix did not see Zeph because he was carrying a large cloth sack of dried berries. The sack was so big the pix couldn't get his arms all the way around it. The lacings had come loose and the mouth was open, the loose sacking flopped around above the pix's head. The little guy dropped the sack with a weary grunt and immediately cried out in dismay, hand reaching futilely to the flapping mouth of the sack that had fallen down to reveal the dried black and blue and red fruit inside.

The pix whirled toward the storm, lifting a hand above his eyes as if doing so would help him see through the rain. Before Zeph could make his presence known, the pix tucked his chin and, arms pumping with effort, dashed out the way he had come.

The pix was gone long enough for the sweet delicious scent of the berries to mingle with the scents of rain and wet earth. Zeph watched the waterdrops splash on the packed dirt before the cleft, studiously ignoring the abandoned foot. The scent of the berries made his stomach rumble.

When had he last eaten? *What* had he last eaten? Cups of ale—all varieties—those he could remember aplenty. And the soft rosy lips that smiled so sweetly while talking him into just one more. One more for her, one more for him, and a flash of bare leg as she slid closer to him. Clever *spreet*. She knew he couldn't resist the long, creamy, nutbrown swell of calf, ...delicate knee, ...the arch of her foot perfection—deliriously so.

And he had told her as much, day after day, while she blushed and batted ink-thickened lashes at him. *Goddess bless*! What had he been thinking?

Gasping for breath and dripping water, the pix returned, a dried, golden berry held between both hands. Carefully, he placed the berry on top of the red, black, and blue ones, then laced the sack closed.

"Where are you taking those?" Zeph wondered out loud.

The pix jumped—little eyes shooting wide and mouth dropping open. Too shocked to say anything, the pix clutched the top of the sack with both hands as if preparing to run.

"Apologies, young pix," Zeph said, tilting his head in a half-hearted bow. "Didn't mean to scare you."

The thundering part of the storm had quieted for a time, though the rain fell steady and strong. Zeph knew the pix could hear him, for the citizens of the Celestial Spires were akin to air, the element that carried their voices, allowing them to converse freely with any of the Goddess's children. An elf—child of the earth and significantly larger than the pix—would need a special spell to translate the high vibrations of pix speak into understandable words. It was possible some elves would need a spell to understand Zeph as well.

In addition to carrying the pix's words to him, Zeph's magic would spin his own words into a higher pitch for the pix's ears to hear.

"I- I didn't know y-you were hhhhere," the pix stammered apologetically.

Zeph shrugged, his wings partially lifting as he did so. This resulted in a more dramatic gasp from the pix who released the death grip on the sack of berries to come a few steps closer.

"You're a- a ssssprityan! I th- th- thought you only aaaaaa spreet."

Zeph lifted a little finger and wriggled it around inside his ear, hoping the pix's erratic stutter was the result of water in his ear interfering with his air magic. "To be fair, the only difference between sprityans and spreets are the wings." He laughed hollowly as the memory of another body—beautiful and his own size—invaded his mind. "Those differences separate us as if by a sky-wide chasm. You have a...." He wasn't sure what pix culture was like. "A girl? Boy?" He scratched the tip of his slightly pointed ear. "Someone you're sweet on?"

"N- n- no." The young pix backed up a step, but he might have been blushing. In the stormlight, it was too difficult to tell.

"Well, sweeties widen the sky-wide chasm from here to the four moons."

A flash of bare leg.

A sweetly curved lip.

The cool ale sliding down his throat and her pressed against his side—until his coin had run dry.

"What are you doing with the berries?" Maybe talking with the youngster would ease the pain inside himself.

"I'm t-taking them across the mmmmmeadow to Ole G- Gran Bbb-rooxlie." The pix's eyes screwed up tightly at the most difficult stutters.

Zeph felt sorry for him. "Your gran's tough on you, is she? Sending you out into the storm." His his own Gran was sharp as a cold north wind and twice as cutting.

"Sh-she's not mmmmy g- gran. That's what eh- vvvvvery one c- calls her."

Surprised, Zeph tilted his head. "Good of you to help her."

The pix lowered his gaze to the packed, sandy dirt and the splotches of wetness where a few lucky drops had fallen through the crack in the top of the cleft. "I- I owe her. It's mmmmy f- f- fault she b- broke her lllleg."

At these words, something hot twisted inside Zeph and his hands curled into fists. Lightning crackled far enough away the thunder was a dull rumble but close enough that the inside of the cleft flashed bright. He could clearly see the pix's petite features.

Head tilted, the pix frowned at the ground. "I wwwwwas r- running from Bbbbig Hoon and Not-so-B- b- big Smilx. They were ch- chasing me fffffffor my capshell." He reached up and touched the acorn shell with fingers as delicate as a dandelion's seed. "I lllllooked b- back to see if I wwwwas g- g- getting away. And I t- tripped ovvvver a root." He cycled his hands in a rolling motion around each other. "I-I-I hit Ole G-gran's bbbbberry stall.".

Zeph didn't want to hear the remainder of the story, but he couldn't stop listening.

The young pix slid to the ground beside his berries, resting his elbows on his knobby knees. "The st- tall fffffell ov- v- ver on her. Her leg bbbbbroke like–" He snapped his slim fingers. "Nnnnnow she c- c-canna g- gather in her own bbbberries."

"Sounds like it wasn't your fault at all," Zeph said. There was a tightness in his chest and anger in voice, an anger he could not control. "Sounds like those other two should be the ones getting caught in a storm with their arms full of berries." As he spoke, he felt heat rising up from his chest and along his neck. His wings trembled, even pressed against the stone as they were.

As if sensing Zeph's reaction to the story, the pix spoke softly, more to himself than Zeph. "M- my Pppppawpaw sa- sa- says, 'If you mmmmake a mmmmess, you c- clean a mess! Th- this is the wwwway you know y- you're ready for your p- place in the wwwworld."

The heat expanded in Zeph's chest. His lips curling even as his head throbbed with inward explosion. Who was this pix to invade the shelter Zeph had found? To speak such words? "Get out."

"Wh-what?" The pix jerked his head up, his eyes enlarging so wide the whites were clearly visible in the grey of the storm.

Thunder rolled as Zeph came to his feet. He lifted his hand and pointed a finger into the rain that was pouring harder now. "Get. Out." And he said it again, all while somewhere inside himself he watched this scene unfolding as if from a distance. He couldn't stop. Couldn't stop the anger. Couldn't stop his wings from trembling with it. Couldn't stop the words which rose in volume and speed just like the thrumming off the rain. "Get out. Get out! GET OUT!"

Three times larger than the little pix, wings spread and a finger pointing like the doom of the Goddess, he must have looked a sight as the lightening flashed, turned the features of his face into a hideous mask.

The pix, his mouth an O of shock and fear, snatched the top of his sack of berries and drug it out into the storm that was thundering again, as if responding to the rage inside of Zeph. A gale swept in and the pix was knocked sideways. He managed to hold on and not fall over, though it was close. Just as he hefted the sack up into his arms, the fickle wind changed. The gale swirled in from another direction. The poor pix was knocked off balance and only managed to remain upright by hopping on one foot. Then, a rain-slick tuft of grass swallowed him up, hiding him from view.

Zeph dropped his arm and felt as if an air draft he had been gliding on had suddenly cut out. He was in a freefall—his entire life was in a freefall—and he didn't know how to stop it. Maybe the heart had wings, wings one could use to fly above the storms of life, or safely through them. But one needed to know those wings existed before one could use them.

He dropped to the floor of the rocky cleft. Water was leaking down the walls in places as the rain found its way through the narrow crack in the top of the rock, damp patches spreading across the sandy dirt. Burying his face in his hands he tried to think, tried to ease the tightness in his chest.

His whole life was one big tumble—falling..., falling..., falling. Followed by a crash into an unexpected obstacles off of which he bounced, only to fall again. He'd lost the ability to right himself in line with the horizon. With the loss of that ability, he did not have any semblance of a destination point.

What had the infuriating pix said? Something about knowing you were ready for your place in the world.

Zeph didn't know what his place in the world was. Couldn't begin to guess. What was he good for? He was good at... flying away and nothing much else. Not a scholar, not a fighter, not a leader. Maybe he was suited to sweep the promenades in the Celestial Spires. Though, all the sweepers he'd ever met were nothing like him. They had a gentle dignity and joy in their task A joy he would never find brush- brush- brushing the glass promenades.

So, *no*, he had no idea what his place in this world might be.

Maybe one had to be ready for that place before it could be

revealed. That sounded like the way the Goddess would think. How, then, did one go about becoming "ready"?

In the calm within his shelter from the storm, he heard again the voice of the little pix, "Make a mess; clean a mess."

Doubt filled his heart and weighed down his limbs. He did not know if he could–

A golden berry, wrinkled in its dried state, flew out of nowhere on the front of a furious blast of wind. It bounced and rolled on the damp sand floor, coming to stop at Zeph's feet. It lay there like evidence presented to the magistrate.

"Your honor, behold this golden berry. Evidence that Zephyrus Shimmerbreeze forced a mere child into a summer storm that threatened his very existence." Zeph could see the imaginary magistrate's mouth turn down in accusation and disgust.

They wouldn't be wrong, though. That little pix could easily get picked up and tossed about just like this berry. The little guy would probably be splattered against a tree in wind like this!

Still doubting himself, Zeph stood up. He might not be able to set right all the other wrongs he'd caused, but he might be able to at least stop another one from happening.

If he could get to the pix in time.

He tensed his flight muscles in and up as tightly as he could, forcing his wings tips down and as directly behind him as possible so that the wind wouldn't catch their edges. Taking a deep breath, he ran out into the storm.

In the space of three rapid heartbeats, he went from "damp" to "dripping wet". Wiping the rain drops out of his eyes with the back of a hand, he squinted at the meadow around him, looking for some sign of the pix. He saw none, so he ran in the direction he'd last seen the little guy go.

The wind was strong, but he tucked his chin in an attempt to keep the rain out of his eyes and still watch the ground and the grass in front of him. The grass was wide-bladed—dark green in the storm. It grew in thick tufts of varying heights interspersed with clusters of ladybells, summer daises, and sun lilies. The petals of the flowers rippled under the assault of the raindrops. Their soft aromas mingled with the wet of the rain and the metallic smell of lightning.

Berries. He smelled squashed berries, their fruity sweetness striking bright notes over the flowers and the storm. He rushed toward their scent, digging in his heels to push against the wind. The berries were scattered on the ground, the sack having torn as it and the pix had been blown against an outcropping of rock jutting like a knobby fist up from the meadow grasses.

The tearing sack was caught on a natural hook in the rock and the pix was holding onto a bunch of the material with one hand. The other was stretched out, trying to grasp the rock itself. His feet were lifted off the ground by the wind rushing over the meadow, bending the grasses and flowers almost flat. A fresh surge of wind pushed the pix harder and the sacking tore away. He was sucked backward by the gale.

Zeph took a hopping step in that direction, his reflexes calculating countless stimuli and the pix's trajectory, and then his back and chest muscles shifted. His wings partially opened, and he was in the air. He let himself tumble a little way, seeking the edge of the thick and powerful stream of air.

While he was battling the winds, a swirling current tossed him higher than he wanted, into the wilder stormwinds. As he struggled to return to the currents closer to the ground, he saw flashes of gold in the darkness of a thorny thicket. Then, a break came—an air current less powerful than the ones around it and Zeph's wings opened without his conscious thought. He caught the current and flew with it.

He put effort into beating his wings as he followed the current downstream. Then through a warmer stream around which and through the colder storm-streams wove. Vaguely, he wondered what it was like to be a being to whom a wind was a single force and not a multi-layered woven tapestry, fluid and in motion.

Then he was straining with the effort of a dive cross- streams. He yawed with every stroke of his wings, adjusting for minute changes in currents, tilting so they wouldn't rip his wings off.

Ahead of him, he could see his target. The pix's mouth was open in a silent scream. Eyes bugging out of his head, even though he couldn't see the tree the wind was hurling him toward. The bark of the sprawling emerald elm was thick and chunky. The pix would easily fit in the chasms between the fat chunks of bark. It would be his vertical grave. He'd become a cautionary tale. The demonstration of why pix children shouldn't be caught out in a storm.

Not if Zeph could help it.

With three strong beats of his wings, he matched speed and direction with the pix. Reaching out, he grasped a handful of the pix's clothes and guided him into an arc, away from his destination.

They came so close to the tree the edge of Zeph's wing scraped the bark. But the pix was safe.

The wind had taken them halfway across the meadow and it was dangerous to attempt to return to the vase. Arms wrapped around the delicate body of the pix, he cast around for some place—any place—that would provide shelter.

There! Something among the tall grasses.

Zeph dove toward the large, wide-mouthed jar, the kind in which elves often stored food items. Perhaps this one had been used at a picnic and had been forgotten as everyone hurried to shelter when the unexpected storm broke.

He landed on the squishy ground by the jar and helped the pix over the lip of the jar's mouth. Then, clambered in after. The glassblower had made the vase well, tinting the glass with amethyst. When lightening lit up the sky, it was as if they were was inside a gem. From the layers of scents inside the glass, the jar had been used to house an arrangement of wildflowers, now blown away.

Zeph guided the shivering pix to the back of the jar and settled down beside him, as the raindrops pounded against the glass, the storm seeking to get at them. Eventually the pix fell asleep, his shivers subsiding. He slid sideways against Zeph's arm.

Zeph dozed but woke with every strong gust that blew like a hollow horn across the mouth of the jar. In time, the wind lessened. The storm passed. And Zeph slept.

IN THE GRAY BEFORE DAWN Zeph woke with stiff muscles and the fear that the revelations of the night before would evaporate in the morning light along with the dew. The urge to slip away from the pix and fly off gurgled in his stomach, a raw, churning need.

He pushed it down. But it wouldn't go away.

The pix woke. He pulled away from Zeph, kept his eyes averted, as if the sprityan was something to terrible to look at.

Struck with shame that his former behavior was the cause of the pix's reaction, Zeph released one of the pouches on his belt, opened it up, and offered the open pouch to the pix at an angle that made it easy to see the flax seeds inside.

"No." Standing up, the pix shook his head and headed toward the mouth of the jar.

"Please, wait, "Zeph said. "I wish to apologize."

The pix paused but didn't turn around. Outside—dawn lit up the drops of water clinging to the grasses. It was as if the goddess had walked through the meadow and sprinkled bright gems everywhere.

Zeph cleared his throat. "What you said, about cleaning up a mess.... Well, I recently made a mess. A mess bigger than a giant's boot."

The pix half-turned.

"I'm Zeph, by the way." He smiled lopsidedly as he fastened the pouch's clasp. "Zephyrus Shimmerbreeze, but my friends call me Zeph."

It seemed that against the pix's own will, his eyes slid to Zeph's wings. Zeph regretted that the first sprityan the pix had met had treated him so poorly. "May I have the honor of your name?"

"N- n- not-as-Bbbig-as-He-Shshshshould-Be Hax," the pix whispered. Even aided by his natural magic, Zeph almost missed the words.

"May I call you Hax?"

"Th- that's me Ppppawpaw."

Zeph nodded in understanding, sprityan names, too, could become unwieldy. "Well, Not-as-Big-as-He-"

"C- c- call me Nnnnobby."

"Nobby, then." Zeph wanted to stand and bow but was afraid towering over Nobby wouldn't send the right message. He bent his head instead. "I humbly ask your forgiveness. I allowed myself to... be... used by someone. A lady spreet. And when she finally cast me away, I—drunkenly—flew out of the tavern and into the face of an oncoming horse." Zeph took a deep breath, remembering the impact on the horse's face, despite being so drunk he couldn't see clearly.

"The horse was harnessed to a noble elf's carriage which overturned into the path of a pumpkin farmer's cart. Squashed pumpkins everywhere. People shouting."

Nobby was facing him now but Zeph looked at the blades of grass pressed against the glass jar. He wished he could reach through the glass and take one of those water droplets. He'd splash it on his shame-hot face. "I... flew away. I was hiding from the Queen's Own Rangers when you had the misfortune of stumbling upon me."

Nobby's eye widened as if he would never consider running from the Queen's Own.

One corner of Zeph's mouth twisted up. "*My* pawpaw taught me many things. But he didn't teach me to clean a mess if I make it." He shrugged one shoulder. "Maybe they did, but I couldn't hear them."

The pix had closed his mouth and he put his hands into the pockets of his shorts as if he didn't know what to say.

Zeph rubbed the palms of his hands on his leggings. "I heard your words. And I do not know my place in the world, but I would like to clean the messes I have recently made." The fear in his belly wriggled around again. "The first mess is the one I made with you. I am sorry."

The pix looked as if he wanted to say all was forgiven. But he scuffed his foot against the glass of the jar. "I lost the berries."

Zeph moved slowly so as not to frighten Nobby. He slid past the pix to the mouth of the jar and then unfolded his eighteen inches to stand. He stretched his shoulders back & forth, feeling his flight muscles loosen. The thicket of golden berries was around here somewhere. Not all that far by flight.

The pix sat on the edge of the jar's mouth, his legs hanging down.

"Will you stay here?" Zeph asked him. "I know where there are some berries."

"Y- you'll come bbbback?" Nobby looked up at the tops of the nearest trees, and around at the meadow grasses, probably trying to figure out where he was in relation to his own home.

Zeph placed his hand on his heart. "I will. And I help you carry your berries to this Gran of yours. Will you allow me to help you?"

At Nobby's nod, he jumped, snapping out his wings and driving them down to gain the height he needed. Soon he spied the berry patch and flew in the direction of the golden berries, the sun of the new day warming his heart.

He was flying but not *away* from something. He was flying toward something. Picking berries and ferrying pixes wasn't his place in the world, but it was a place to start.

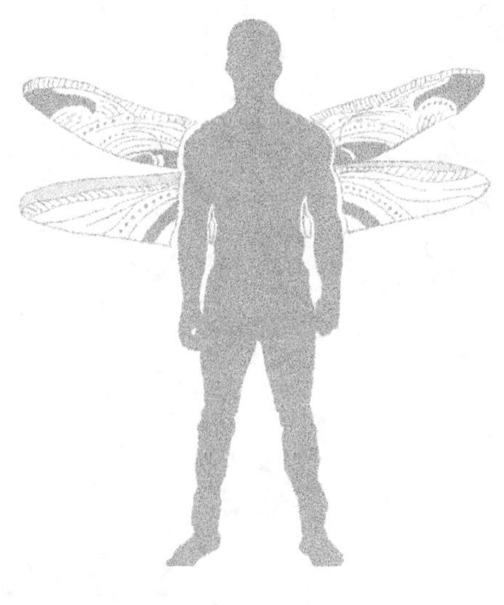

Our fourth story springs from the creative soul of our Unnerving Fairy who watches over small animals, fountain pens, and sparkling things. With an unusual take on this #minithology's theme, she weaves a story of a girl who doesn't quite fit in and a fairy encounter who won't soon forget.

THE RATH OF SHELTER ISLAND

Tracy Eire

THROUGH CROSSINGS UNTOLD, AND BOROUGHS *boundless, I've fought my way to this island....*

She thought the words idly.

In fact, she listened to distant thunder, the telltale cobalt speckling of rain, and, like most, felt lulled by the occasional squeak of air brakes and the diesel-wake of the bus's passage. But, unlike most, it caused a deep resonance inside of Trudy Tough.

She could become as quiet and still *inside* as a stone. And it was because there was no easy and comfortable explanation forthcoming for this that *she* was *here*. Trudy didn't know what pulled her moods out like the edges of bedsheets or like the tides that circumnavigated the island she was on, just off the coast of New York state. Through no fault of her own, she wasn't much like her sporty and dreamy sisters Amy and Vera. Childless Ross and Ericka had taken all three of them on from different places.

It showed up in their looks. Amy was a tall, heroic Artemis, with dark brown skin and eyes, thick dark hair, and she'd spoken Spanish as far back as she could remember. Vera was pale and grey-eyed, like Minerva, but plump and romantic, like Venus. But Tru was skinny. Quiet. Brown haired and dark eyed. Even when they'd first carried her into their lives, too small to walk, she'd had *the stillness* inside. And she was given to bouts of such deep quiet and unnerving hush that her less than delighted parents had taken her for testing.

Yeah. There was no 'goddess' for Tru.

And other people chased a phantom misconfiguration in her system to this day.

Off to her left, lightning crawled the sky followed by a terrific *crack*, as it shattered what it sought to find. Tru tucked a hand under her chin, possibly the only warm body on the bus who *hadn't* jumped when that had happened.

This invitation was the absolute *culmination* of months of work. Trudy was determined to see it go right. So! She reminded herself to jump. To react. To be *just like* all the others.

She was still afraid it would go wrong somehow—that her phone would ring and she'd be yanked out of the bus and thrust back on the ferry she'd just crossed water on. Dragged back home by a magnet.

She'd fought the good fight through test after test and deserved the R&R of being here.

And *here* was... a nondescript crossroad in trees.

Tru checked her phone against the street signs again. On all sides, wide walkways and tall trees insured privacy. But also meant that someone entering this world for the first time wouldn't really *have* anywhere to turn for help. She wasn't sure if that was exciting... or not.

She came to her senses in the rather upscale bus and shot to her feet. "*Right*. Of course."

The bus had sloshed to a stop against a cobbled curb, and Tru was left no choice but to snatch the handle of her rolling bag and head down the exit stairs. This bag that was heavier *by the mile*, she swore. The doors swished open.

As she stepped out onto the curb and looked up into a patchwork of scattered breaks, the bus pulled away. Between squalls, and the flutters of her midi-dress, she watched sun paint the land around her with great golden brushes, and for the first time in years, had nothing to fall back on but promises.

There was no one to meet her.

Tru lingered to look up at the moving clouds around her, until, at last, the grey plafond above broke open to gold, and she stood with her face upturned, stroked by sable rays no differently than any tree, stone, or turret in their path. But, of course, *very differently* too.

Then she shut her eyes in a sudden moment of stalled momentum – the sort of thing her parents warned of, complained of, *dragged her to a dozen psychologists* because of, and had monitored on calendars like a mental defect. Because, for several beats, Tru was elsewhere, deep inside the sun.

And for the first time in ages... there was no one there to stop–

"Hey! About time you got here, loser!" Said the girl who emerged from an SUV some feet away. Tru heard and felt the world, again, and turned her head.

Audrey. Her friend looked a little flustered. She was, Tru thought, embarrassed at her lateness, but *ever chic* in her neat leather heals, blush frilled blouse, and pink plaid wrap-around skirt as she popped out of the SUV. She didn't even bother to open the little clear umbrella whose handle was adorned with a pink fabric bow, even though the sun began to pass.

"Audrey!" Tru felt a smile crease her features. It was *her* summer home Tru's parents had agreed to send Tru to *haunt*. Not that the girls knew one another outside of school. Or not *yet*. But they worked well together, and had hit it off quickly.

It was impossible to call Audrey 'bougie', since that implied that Audrey knew *middle-class* from *demi-glace... au poulet*. And she *didn't*. But that was *okay*. She was a Carnegie Hill blueblood as well-off as silver spoons came. Born more than a stone's throw from the Toughs of Cobble Hill, though Tru's family was quite comfortable now. Toughs always lived in Brooklyn, Tru's father joked as if this were elemental, but the addresses got more 'respectable'. They were a bridge away from Manhattan now, squeezed up near the water's edge.

Money was like gravity.

"Well, *come on*." Audrey beckoned. "We don't stand on ceremony here, Tru. This is *Shelter Island*, not *Schwinghammer Prep*."

"Then why aren't you in jeans and a tee-shirt?" Tru gestured at her friend. *Jeans* might cause Audrey to *dissolve*.

"I don't, uhm, own... those things?" Audrey shook out dark and dramatic waves of hair, far too perfect for the wind, and looked at her feet. "Truey! We need to *get going*, not *go shopping*. You're *late*, which means *I'm late*. And that's a problem. It's *my* get-together, at *my* place."

She checked her big round watch.

"Okay, *touché*." Tru wheeled herself over at a trot, folded down her luggage handle, and aimed for the trunk of the car. It plainly *confused* the driver who stood at the back and hesitated by the curb.

"Let go the bag, *genius.*" Audrey laughed before she vanished back into the new-car scent of the S.U.V.

Tru handed off her bag with a *Thank You.*

Inside was spacious and spotless, all the plush leather surfaces were two-tone: taupe and chocolate brown. Tru belted in as the trunk shut behind her. *Yeeouch, pricy.* She worked the sliver of switch to roll down the window just to be sure she knew what it was, and then tried to look casual. "The ferry over was *hectic.* Did you get delayed?" Tru wouldn't dare mention the people who'd been puking all around her.

Audrey stopped fixing her lipstick and clacked the compact shut, "I arrived thirty-four minutes ago. I knew you were coming in on the ferry. *I'm sorry* we weren't waiting when you got to the crossroads, Tru. We actually had to take the private airstrip."

"There's a private airstrip?" Tru's eyes widened.

"Of *course.* It's not far from the stables." Audrey nodded at her.

Well. Tru had never been *near* a horse, but in some Neolithic cobweb of her brain she liked the *idea* of horses.

Thick privacy trees with long cobbled drives blinked by as they drove well-groomed roads.

Glimpses of houses *so large* that Trudy had only seen the like of them on television before.

She wasn't in Brooklyn anymore.

It was justifiable that she heard only bits and bobs of Audrey's urbane transatlantic accent. Words about long beaches. Private pools. Daily riding. Country Clubs. Tru's brows bunched together.

She wasn't plucked from the breast of an eighteenth century poetic like her sister Vera was, but Tru always did her research. The land had been Algonquian. The land had become a Plantation operated by slaves. Tru's big sister was Black girl. But none of it connected for Audrey. History never appeared in her recounting. "-and twenty-five thousand people in the off season. However, this *is* summer holiday. Expect at least eight thousand people making themselves at home, and, for the first time, you'll be one of them! Isn't that exciting?"

Still, Tru found it hard to look away from the streets, "The houses look like *hotels*."

Audrey laughed as she settled back in her seat. "You're going to have great fun."

The Dublin Retreat was a brick, Federal-style manse, spacious and *beautiful*. At their arrival? Cherry lemonade. Lobster rolls. Then tea and a cup of seasonal berries in crème anglaise.

In a place that was *not* average. The brick house had three floors and twelve bedrooms, coffers on all the recessed ceilings, and gorgeous fireplaces against the night air, which was still chill. And it turned out that Tru and Audrey were *early*. There were two more girls, and *four* guys, all of whom were in *some* state of arriving, as they walked out of the dining room.

By the time the staff locked the doors for the night, Trudy had gotten reacquainted with Audrey's best friends, also students at Schwinghammer Prep. Chantal Langone had French-Canadian parents, and the kind of accent one might imagine of a girl who spent half her time in Murray Hill Park, Montreal. Ava Peltz, like Trudy, was something of an up-and-comer, but from the upper West Side. And the more of these people Tru experienced, the more she wondered what she was doing on Shelter Island to begin with.

It seemed *too* lucky.

Only one of the invited boys arrived that night. Audrey's boyfriend, Roderick Clin, who came in from the weather dotted with seawater. Tall, handsome, Captain-of-the-squad type. In his case, the sport was *water-polo*.

He'd stood by the fire screen in the massive front room and tried not to be seen shivering.

"Oh. Wait. This is her?" Roderick's eyes were almond-shaped and upswept at the outside edges. His smile was bright in his dark face as he caught himself and redirected to her. "Tru Tough?"

"Yes."

He actually laughed. "It's a pleasure to meet you. I've heard a lot."

Rod was big and warm and full of life. His attention was flattering. Kind of.

Tru felt a bit exposed.

At Schwinghammer Prep, she was Audrey's Chemistry and Biology lab partner, and even lab admins noticed how they communicated and cooperated well. They worked quickly and efficiently together, with occasional grinning and mutual eyerolls thrown in – they were teenaged girls, after all.

Was that enough to justify... *this place*?

Then what could justify such a place as this?

Rod returned his attention to Audrey soon enough. "Win, Rupert, and Blaine are on the last ferry. It's possible they were held up by weather. There are storms along the coast." He indicated the many water-streaked window panels across from them. When he glanced at Tru he said, "Call me Rod."

He was honestly so handsome in person that it was a little *breathtaking*. Rod was an excellent match to Audrey, who stood on her toes to give him a peck on the mouth, so as to welcome him at the same time as she didn't scandalize her guests.

That's how it was done in these parts.

The thunderstorm rolled into Gardiner's Bay, burst ashore, and spent its fury in the wetlands that night. And while it did, Tru spent many hours gliding out of her assigned room to take photos of the house for Vera. She zipped and sent pictures twice near one AM after she'd found a period *loom* in one massive room, and a nineteenth century treadle sewing machine, its shape slender and black. Her sister's poetical heart would shatter and reshape itself around stories of this place, Tru felt sure.

She fell heavily asleep, phone in hand, at two AM. Then her consciousness floated between four posts of a lavish bed, aware only of the bellowing storm beyond the walls. It raced along the twenty-four miles of island with the occasional crack of its heavy hoofbeats in the sky, with not a soul outside to witness it. And it put Tru on edge.

At three AM, she woke when all the sounds she was still growing accustomed to—the sounds of systems that were automated in modern houses—stopped at once. This coincided with a tremendous *flash-crack* close by the house. Tru, who was still fully dressed on top of the sheets, sat up into the rainy darkness. The power had gone out, and beyond it, she could hear the sounds of the island, as naked as it had been born and lived, for centuries. There was nothing but walls and panes of glass between the downpour, thundering ocean, and the storm that barged along the heath.

Tru rolled to her phone in the sheets and flicked it on to a *No Service* message.

Thank you, weather. My charger is dead.

At least she'd gotten photos to Vera.

She curled, too shaken to get up and undress in the flickering room.

Besides, it would be getting colder soon enough.

When the door tapped, Tru fairly skittered off the bed and under it. *How was that for 'reacting'?*

"Trudy?"

The voice was Audrey's, so Trudy got up, smoothed her clothes, and went to greet her. The girl stood in a long lavender housecoat, with a candle on an honest-to-the-nineteenth-century brass candle dish. And it was just too much to ask for Tru to swing up her camera and get some tight shots of this antique contraption for Vera. Audrey sure looked startled enough at finding Tru *fully dressed*. "*My goodness*! Are you... wet? Have you been *outside*?"

"No." Trudy confessed. "It's a bit spooky outside."

"Then I'm glad I came to check on you." Said the other girl. "The power's out. If you haven't tried a switch. But we're all awake – it's a bit of a tradition on the first night. No one wanted to bother you since... most 'people are asleep."

"*All awake*?" Yet Tru hadn't seen a *soul* while wandering the house to take photos.

"Yes. Over in my suite, but... I thought it might be a good time to check on you and go to the kitchen for snacks." A wisp of smoke coiled up from her candle and vanished in the dark.

Trudy stepped out and shut her door. "The power is out. There's no way to make anything."

"*Make*? We won't *make* anything. No." Said the girl. "There are cherry pies in the chiller, and the ice-cream is hand-churned here."

The hallway was illuminated by electric blue lights. She could see the tall shape of Roderick at the far end by the stairs, as he awaited Audrey, and as considerate as the boyfriendly gesture was, it made Tru judder to suddenly see him there in the dark. The inside of her brain slowed the moment. Went *still* on it. She shook that out of her head.

He probably didn't want Audrey to take on the huge staircase without a way to see the steps before her. Or, like with the shivering, he was afraid of the dark, himself.

"Come on," Rod said as reassuringly as he could to them both. "But let's be careful on the steps. I hear there's pie."

Near the kitchen, the light that rounded the corner was Chantal, who now stood in the white arch of doorway. She scanned Tru over and said, "Trudy? I can assure you, as loud as this storm is, it won't drive us off the island and to the coast. You can go to bed. Well. After the pie."

Ava appeared from a kitchen nook and held up a fork. "Didn't you hear me? The *filling* is *still warm*." She vanished back again.

In the white-walled dining room, someone had shoved aside the centerpiece vase full of peonies and replaced it with a large, lattice-topped cherry pie. Audrey stood working out how to cut the massive thing with the piddling butterknife that had been on the sideboard. While Ava debated slice sizes. They were so strange, like they had no experience serving up treats at all. Rod stuck a spoon into the lattice and pulled out a chunk. Tru snatched up a fork to do the same.

Warmth and cherry tartness burst along her tongue. On the top of the thick and flaky crust there were granules of sugar, and it was deliciously fresh.

"Stop-stop-stop!" Audrey waved the butter-knife and cried.

"No-no-no!" her boyfriend replied with a cake-eating grin.

He turned to Tru, reached out, and the handles of their flatware crossed in a celebratory clang before each of them set in again.

Soon enough candles glowed around their bent figures as they downed pie and slurped from cans of coffee or energy drink, and Rod, who had started early, got up to light the fireplace at the end of the elegant room. Looking out the bow-topped windows, reverberations of thunder began to lap strokes of lightning. Ava paused in her recitation of the trip across Noyack Bay to count the interval. "It's at the door." She said. The rain became savage at the window panes.

"I was lucky to arrive when I did." Chantal extended a hand to the fire. "I can only think of Blaine in some hotel room in North Haven tonight, instead of here, and warm, with me. Poor thing."

"But *safe*. And he'll be along soon enough," Audrey comforted her friend.

Rod noted, "And he's missing you. It's actually *annoying* to talk to him. Same with you, Ava. Rupert is downright aggravating. He's composing *doggerel*."

"Oh. I know from doggerel," Tru piped. There were few things Vera hated more. And even her big sister, Amy, who'd once professed herself allergic to bombast, could respect that. Tru set a hand on her breast and waved her fork for emphasis. "Oh, storm you are so dangerous / your rain clouds do not favour us / For the power in this house is gone out / and that makes us flounder about / in a dark / that is just like men's hearts."

Chantal wasn't the only one to burst into laughter.

"Not bad. Not bad." Said Rod.

Audrey made a delicate scoff, "Well, hon, I'd like to hear you do better."

Rod squared up, his expression taking on a brow-wrinkling erudition that made them all roar with laughter, and he set in. "Weather... you are unfair / why must you charge across the land / from rooftop, to blacktop, to strand?"

That gained some *ooohs* from them.

Tru chuckled to Audrey, "I think you should have challenged him to do *worse*."

"Oh me! Me!" said Chantal excitedly. "Let's see.... Great Bull on this cracking night / out upon the highlands and the fen / wild with grief and keening / your shouts have come again."

The candles in the room guttered a sudden left upon the table and it startled Tru...

... until Ava stood up and fastened a window that had come lose from its latch.

"Scaring up ghosts in a still room, Chantal?" Ava sighed. "So very *Gallic*."

"In a still room full of *warm pie*, is *inconsideration*," Audrey condemned.

"Who is the Great Bull?" Tru asked.

This was met by silence and turned heads.

Then Audrey shook out her loose hair, nearly dislodging the ribbon over her crown. "Oh, it's a... it's a Shelter Island wives' tale, I grew up with. Almost all of us heard of it from spending holidays over here. Nothing but a bugaboo to get the children inside before dark is all."

By shifting her gaze around the table, Tru could see they were all, now, a little leery, a touch more nervous. Tru thought this was great fun for a stormy night and nodded over her canned coffee. "Then tell me about the Great Bull? What's the story?"

For a second or two, no one moved. And then Rod set up with a great roar of *BOO!*

Every soul, even Rod, she suspected, jolted in surprise, and then burst out laughing.

Tru hadn't moved. But no one had noticed.

The lights flicked on, which led to another outcry. The kitchen maid came squinting and blinking in from the attic quarters and shook her head reproachfully at the lot of them. Between them, they'd demolished a cherry and a raisin pie. The middle-aged woman didn't at all look surprised.

All-in-all, it was great fun! But Tru was well-tired of running her tongue over the sugar on her teeth, so, she made her blurry way to her bedroom toothbrush. Even the iced-coffee couldn't keep her brain awake. As she was crossing through the hall, she heard, somewhere below her, the sound of people arriving.

IN THE NEXT DAYS, AS she got to know Rupert, Blaine, and Winston, Tru forgot about storm and bullock alike. Shelter Island rolled out its great green carpet of welcome to an influx of people, many teens who had nightly gatherings around campfires on beaches Tru had once *longed* to tread. A few days further on, and she realized she hadn't worn shoes *in a week.*

Dawn came? Tru went out back, onto the beach. She searched for rounded sea glass to twist into copper jewelry, sunbathed with her friends in a Chinook of fair weather, collapsed with books, read aloud, took her meals, all on the beach behind Audrey's vacation house.

The beach was the life in this place.

In this exceptional bird-call stillness, she stole time and space to simply sit, wrapped in sand, and go completely silent under the stars. Whenever she sank into that peculiar state, her body held faithful position on some three feet of earthly geography, while the rest of her was *far* from the world. It wasn't as if she reminisced or daydreamed. Tru didn't know what to call it. Slowly, that peace descended into her bones. She walked in and out of it like a revolving door. But one she'd never been granted the grace to learn to use.

This fulfilled her in ways she couldn't even relate to. She'd flit back from the faraway to find the hummingbirds gliding by, almost at eye level, often with their long beaks in a red, floral feeder that dangled from a wrought iron stake in the sand.

She stretched in early sun.

Amy was nigh unto a sports star at Ithaca.

Vera was being scouted by Juilliard.

Tru had the *most useless* form of genius ever.

She opened her arms and thought: *Behold. My. Stillness. And tremble.*

Then laughed aloud at herself.

AUDREY HAD BEEN RIGHT.

Soon the island filled up.

The night air was thick with smoke and bonfires as huge wood piles of oceanic detritus sent sparks up in the night sky, like flags against stars that didn't recognize their nations. Tru, very much a fixture at these firesides, felt the strange beachy energy in the bare soles of her feet a few hours before the evening came. She was always excited as she watched the burn barrels and fires getting laid in with wood and kindling.

She bounced on her toes until it was dark enough that the first fingertips of flame touched off a blaze. That night, she abandoned all pretense and hung out in the kitchen nook, and when the first matches fell, she shut the book she was reading aloud, and fairly charged out through the back door.

"Hey, wait!" Audrey, her hair in little short braids behind her ears, raced with her.

Rod was already prodding the Dublin bonfire to life, his expression nearly beatific as Win and Blaine threw on driftwood. It was the presence of wet wood that sent up so much smoke, but in the still air, they made pillars to the cumulus, one-thousand feet up.

Chantal nudged her. "Are you gonna dance? A little bird told me you can dance."

"You can't?" Tru was startled. She shook herself, realizing that was probably Chantal being kind. The French-Canadian girl would have lessons, just... not in anything modern. "What little bird was that?"

"Well." Blaine's brows swept up over his beer. "Who's missing?"

"Who's missing?" What a strange question. Yet, even as she looked around —at Rod and Blaine opening beers, Audrey pinning her hair, and Ava stretching in the slowly cooling air.

Tru got to her feet in the hale smell of burning wood.

"That little bird," Chantal told her playfully.

Win. Winston Weber. Tru had spent a few nights dancing with him because he seemed as goofy as she did about it. And he was fun. He had black, loosely curling hair, blue eyes, and pale skin, slightly flushed wherever the sun and wind reached it regularly. He was a bit like the hummingbirds that drew her attention on the edge of this beach. They lived in the walled gardens inside, mostly—large eyed, and full of nervous energy. Win was the opposite of her deep gulf of stillness.

And, *yeah*, it *was* fun to dance with him.

It was a bit of a downer to face the night without him.

A blot on what was an otherwise perfect time.

"I'll find him," Tru told her friend.

She walked toward the ever-present of delectable food on the table. Audrey and Rod were, at the moment, not to be disturbed right then, so she detoured around them. Tru came out around the point and could see... bonfires for miles. It was *magical*.

She started walking because she didn't find him. It was a quarter of a mile before she saw him, head down, hands in his long short's pockets. The breeze flicked both his dark curls and the edge of the plaid shirt he wore over his tee. He kicked a clod of sand as he walked in her direction and seemed to have a lot on his mind.

He didn't look up, so as she passed him, Tru said, "Something bugging you, Win?"

It was funny to watch him jolt in place like he'd had an electric shock. Tru laughed.

Win didn't speak to her for once, he just watched, like the bird often did. She turned to walk in the direction he'd been going, back toward Audrey's fire. Then Tru glanced his way. "I'm here because I'm Chantal's friend. And she wanted someone to find you."

"Oh. Okay, thanks for telling me." Winston nodded.

"Not to dance. Or be your plus one," She explained.

"No. I... okay. I didn't ever think so." He acknowledged with a sudden near-smile.

There was a long pause of walking during which he returned to being comfortable in her echoic silence. Then Tru glanced across at him. "The night's still cold between fires."

He took the plaid shirt off and offered it to her, and Tru took it gratefully. Then Win caught her shoulders and veered. He had to help her keep her footing as sand spat up to her thighs, splashed against her white denim shorts and over-sized tee. She'd been narrowly missed by a shirtless drunken guy who charged along the wide beachfront wearing a big, rubber, bull's mask over his head. The horns bobbed up a down like elongated cow dugs as he bellowed and snorted. Other guys chased him, shaking their beers, and spraying him to drive him along.

"*Idiots.*" Win chuckled.

"The Great Bull." She remembered.

"You know that's kiddy stuff." He told her. "Besides, it's supposed to be unlucky to talk about it. To even notice it." He tried to change the subject to one of Tru's faves. "Do you want some pineapple? They're grilling it with some pigs. The meat is local, and the rest is organic."

Tru had discovered a week ago that she was *always* up for grilled pineapple. It surprised her when they sat filling their faces, and licking pineapple juice off their hands, that Win started to tell her the story *unprompted.*

"Y'know they say every few years that... this Bull turns up on the island again, tearing around looking for something, like mad. There was this Scottish farmer who sailed all the way to the new world to bury this bone in a jar. And then he turned around and went home. All of a sudden, Shelter Island has this *Great Bull.* It must find the bone. Or, those are the rumours. The... perfectly hor-rible rumours." He paused and shook his head. "But it's, you know... it's stupid, fairy tale stuff."

"That's a wild story." She sucked a fingertip. "Where did it come from?"

"You know, I don't know?" Win rubbed his forehead. "There's supposed to be a way to stop it too. Like people have said you have to throw down grain in front of it, and it will stop and eat it, but... I just..." he paused to laugh.

Tru nodded. "Like stories about throwing down seeds in front of vampires, right? That they'll stop to count it? That's just human anxiety trying to find a way to ease itself. If vampires were real, and really hunting, and really cornering you, they wouldn't care about counting anything."

Win nodded and got to his feet. "For sure. It's... it's what you say. That explains why there're supposed to be spells, and trinkets, and all kinds of stuff to save you from it. There's a saying Audrey learned when she was a kid, and it's meant to protect you from it. Lots of people around here know it. *Seven years I've looked for you. Searched the sand dunes to find you. I brought you this white shirt to wear, to take you safely out of here....* Something like that."

Tru found it interesting. "*You* know it."

"I... used to summer here too. Her nanny taught it to us." He admitted.

"Seven years." She exhaled and counted time. She was 17. She'd been in therapy learning to supress... whatever it was that was *wrong* with her thinking, for seven years. That was a long time to scramble around these white dunes looking for someone. "Any truth to it? Maybe some history?"

"That... is where it gets weird, actually. But it shouldn't be me telling it." Then he reached for his drink and pulled a long swallow. "I know descendants of a person who saw it. *They* should tell you the story." He drank again.

Minutes later Winston Weber brought her in to sit at a huddled fire in a cove draped by trees. There, people sat in closer conversations, the atmosphere was more chill. It suited Tru well enough. And it would up until the eating was done and the music started.

But she noticed that, at this fire, a pair of young African American artists were turning faces into tigers, butterflies, and bouquets. Tru watched this in fascination, up until Win went to them and bent to talk to the young man. His paint-smeared hand lifted a rock from a small cairn so that Win could set down a few bills. The young man pinned them under the makeshift piggybank again.

As soon as the girl they were working on was done, her skin vibrant with a pink peony opening on her forehead, and orange butterfly wings nestled against her lower eyelids, the young African American woman noted, "Where is this girl? Is it you?"

She gestured at Tru, who got up and glanced over at Win. "Who's this?"

His lips flattened in a smile. "You want to know about the Great Bull? Hear them out."

The young man artist started shifting paint pots around. The girl beside him cleaned her brushes in soap and rinsed them in salt water before she set in. "You paid for the story?" Said the young woman with a sigh. "Sit down."

They didn't ask if she wanted to have leopard spots, or a nebula, or a dusting of tiny yellow stars on the tops of her cheeks—though she might have liked that last. Almost like a string section, they paused, poised, and then set in as one. For a few moments, neither spoke, then the girl said, "You have nice, smooth skin for this."

Tru tried not to move as Win sat down beside her.

"Ah. Stay still now." The young man rubbed some kind of light gel into her skin, "To get the story, you need to head backwards in time. You have to imagine how isolated this island was. Cut off like a ship in a bottle. But most people can't do that, so we ask them to close their eyes and think."

Close her eyes?

"If you have to move, let me know." Said the young woman artist. Then she started in. "There's a reason why Winston brought you over here. Our family was brought to this place, *way* back, before we were a free people. Back to generations when we owned nothing, had nothing, were allotted fabric, and raised chickens in secret to sell across the bay."

"Like a side hustle, except the whole situation was –" Tru's lips compressed.

"Don't talk. It moves your face," said the young woman. "Just *listen*. We can't *change* the past. Much as we all want to change the past. I'm just trying to get you to *see* it."

Tru shifted gears.

See it.

"This was 1651," said the young woman, "The island didn't know much about the world yet. Just the Native groups of people who called it home. Half of my family came from Barbados, in 1651. We came by sea, jammed in the bottom of boats, and it wasn't pretty."

Win shifted beside her, and the young Black man's voice punctuated. "Sit still, ants-in-your-pants." This threatened to make Tru chuckle. She just barely caught herself.

To see, she had to focus.

"Shelter Island was what's called a provisioning plantation. In this place, crops and animals were raised up, kept healthy, and the whole island made fruitful every year, by the grace of Mother Nature, and the ingenuity of slaves. This island was the work of Old-world tribes, meeting New."

Tru listened and reached into the stillness to move backward in time. Though she knew it wasn't possible to do such a thing. The outside world fell away.

"At the end of the cycle, crop and cow alike would be cut down, boxed up, and shipped across the ocean, back to sugar plantations in Barbados," said the young Black woman, "My family kept the cows here. Birthed the calves. It was us who made sure they survived. That's what my family did."

Tru's consciousness twigged to the onset of harvest. It spread its orange leaves out upon the island where pumpkins ripened, animals huddled, and slaves had to maintain the very industry that oppressed them. This image shifted to towering seas churning a rudder so that spray leapt in the wind. Supplies headed for the slavers in Barbados – a cog in a cruel system. Tru could feel herself going under, because the next words the young artist said, were more image than speech.

"The land gave us its secrets. Over time we knew every waterline, every rising up, and falling down around here, like breathing. Just imagine living your entire life within twenty-four miles of your front door. First, you're born on it. Then you're exploited. Finally, you're buried under it. You'd get to know it. And we got to know it well."

Salt water sloshed as the young woman cleaned her brush, but Tru didn't hear it. Her eyes were overlooking seasons changing in this place as if she could stand there, ageless as a tree, and watch it from the outside.

The girl spoke on, "About half the island's swamp. Today, it's a preserve. But back then, our families just said that the lamps we lit, the fires that that dotted our hearths, had a twin sitting over in the dark. That came to a head one winter. One of my relatives went out on the fen after a cow who'd broken out of her hobbles. It was freezing. The dead of winter. Or so it was written down. He went into the heart of the fen to find her. And there was... a clearing dotted with only a few big, broad trees. And in that clearing, between those trees, was a horseshoe ditch. And inside the horseshoe ditch, was a mound sitting there. All under fat flakes of snow coming down."

The air felt hard and crisp. Tru's thoughts pushed through scrub, the smell of pine, on into a sudden clearing. The great grassy... cellar stood up from a sunken trench in thick snowfall, dark and foreboding. It looked like a fragment out of myth—the tomb of a paleolithic monarch. Tru's eyes couldn't seem look away. Her ears caught the frantic low of the cow out there *some-where* in the trees, so that her head turned toward the sound, and back, to land on this... great pair of glowing eyes.

Tru jolted back to the party. Her senses all opened on the smells of wood burning, the soothing firelight darkness, the sound of waves rolling, Win, warm beside her – all of it rushed into the space where the snow, pine, and fen had been. The young Black woman's brush had paused in air. Her brows pinched together a little as she tried to reason out what had startled Tru.

What?

Tru was stunned. She shut her eyes and tried to see the place again. *Something* could make sense of... whatever paranoia had made her think she saw *big, burning eyes.*

The girl went on, "On the mound there was a bull, easily taller than a man. Several thousands of pounds. The history isn't clear on this, some say it was red, and some say it was black, but there was a *great bull* on the mound, with massive horns, hooves like stones, and burning eyes that stared at the edge of the clearing like it couldn't see a way out. It had been trapped there, waiting on the mound, inside the ditch, inside the clearing, inside the fen, on this island. He should have heard it breathing, or seen some motion of it moving in the snow. But it had just suddenly... been there. It made no sound. No motion. Well. My relative backed away, *turned*, and *ran*. And when he found the cow, *she* was running for home too. They fled through the whole night together, yet they didn't make it back *till dawn*. And the whole way, he said it was behind him."

The brush lifted at last.

The artist finished, "Because now, it was free."

Tru's eyes rolled open naturally this time. At that moment, she didn't have a clue what was painted on her face, but that wasn't even a consideration. For the first time in her life... she thought she'd *seen something* in the great, echoing stillness *inside*. Tru rose and brought both hands up to the sides of her head.

"Trudy? You okay?" Win asked her. "Tipsy?"

The young artist got to her feet to steady Tru. "Win... take her back to Audrey's and get her a cup of coffee, okay? I think she's had a bit too much." She bundled them and got them moving away.

But not before the other artist stood and called after them, "Every few years, the Bull takes someone, and they are never seen again. Be careful out there, both of you. We are overdue."

Slave labour. And monsters. What a great vacation spot, Audrey.

Still, there *was* nothing else *in* that space where Tru went. *Ever.* How had the eyes happened?

Win had the grace to collect her and steer her back toward Audrey's house, even as she trudged, confounded, trying to work her way into to that altered state she'd *never* reach given how rattled she was.

Win sprinted a little ahead as Audrey came from the fireside. It was possible to hear a sudden spat of debate between the pair of them.

Audrey threw up her hands, "*What* is she doing with *that* painted on her forehead?"

The wind kicked a sudden flutter of fire to snap like a sail in air. Tru couldn't hear the first words that Win said. But she could make it out quite clearly when he turned his head and said, "I think they really scared her."

"I'm *fine*." She reached up and swabbed her forehead with her bare fingertips, the pads of each finger became a smear of dark paints. "Whatever it is, uh, I can wash it away. Don't worry about it."

"*Wash it. Away?*" Audrey said sharply to Win.

Tru made a detour for the house, whose back doors were unlocked.

In the washroom off the kitchen, she flipped on the light and started the water running.

When her gaze flicked upward, what she saw initially chilled her, but then... it made her grin. "That girl has some mad skills." She smiled as she swabbed away a rather excellently rendered pair of red animal eyes that had been painted on a dark and snowy sky. They had stared out from just above her own eyebrows.

"Trudy?" Audrey drifted to the door with Rod trailing off behind her. "You okay?"

"*Oh*, the Force is strong with that artist," Tru noted as she scrubbed paint away.

Audrey was tipsy, but more concerned than ever, "What are you talking about?"

Rod swept a hand over his face. "Babe, *The Force*. You know –" and he made rather decent light saber sounds as he pretended to swing one in air, "– *Thee* Force."

"I know what Star Wars is, Rodrick," Audrey said flatly. Then she turned to Tru again, her voice much more understanding, "But what *Force* do Remy and Ramona Burg have?"

"The power of *suggestion*." Tru soaped her forehead with a cloth. "Ramona paints eyes, and, you know, sitting there with my own shut—I think I see *eyes*. Well, *of course* I do. I can *feel* the *shapes* her brush is making on my forehead." Tru laughed and sketched what she considered a wizarding gesture. "It's *magic*."

Audrey noted, "Truey that *bar of soap* isn't a *magic wand*. And if you keep waving it around it'll shoot out of your hand into the bidet. That happens? *I'm not getting it.*"

"Right-right." Tru winced and set it down in the little bronze seashell again. She gave her long hands a final wash, dried off, and then walked back outside with an arm looped through Audrey's. Music had begun at last, and she was soon circling the flames with abandon.

Within the hour, however, fat raindrops began to extinguish all the fires they'd built.

And, likewise, Tru didn't realize she had no idea what *real* magic *actually* looked like.

EVERY FEW YEARS, THE BULL *takes someone. And they are never seen again.*

Tru woke in the softness of Egyptian cotton sheets, with birds singing in air so fresh that it reached through the screens and curled on the comforter under which she lay, lulled by their weight.

Last night, they'd all vanished into their rooms by midnight. It had been a long day of partying and some of them had red-eyed 'tipsy' in their rear-view mirrors. Tru showered, curled her hair, and she was still the first and only of them outside. The staff set out chopped fruit with cream, and fresh biscuits. They knew her by now. *Everything* had a dusting of organic sugar.

She brought the bowl inside when she'd finished up.

Surprisingly, the three staffers in the kitchen all stood distractedly around the kitchen TV screen that usually displayed the weather and time—or always had when *Tru* had been there to look in on it. She set the bowl on the sideboard and went to brush her teeth. When she passed by the kitchen minutes later, two more people, the beachcombers who cleaned the ocean's debris from the vacation home shoreline, and who worked everyone around here, were inside. Normally, they wouldn't have dared to have anyone to think them idle. They were both retired and knew how to work. But they were so fixed on the TV, Tru drifted into the room and almost stood between where they forgot their fresh cups of hazelnut roast.

Then she backed out of the room quietly and went in search of a television.

She hadn't watched television since her arrival here, but she had spotted a few of them on her first night drifting through Audrey's beach house. On the second floor, in a sitting room off the sewing room there was a television.

It gave her some pause that there was a stack of linen now sitting by the one of the more modern sewing machines—someone planned to use the machine today—but the little television room with its fourty-inch flatscreen tucked away in one corner, was empty.

She smoothed her hair back, caught up the remote, and turned it on. Then Tru stood by the trio of chairs there and stared.

She shut the television off when the report looped and she realized she'd been standing for close to forty-five minutes. Then she trotted down the hall to knock on Audrey's door. There was no answer, so running through the expanse of the girl's room, which took a moment, as there was a suite involved, she could see her friends out on the beach. The boys seemed to be searching the grassy dunes. The girls trudged along bare-legged and still chilly, their hair blowing.

This great house had been in Audrey's family for two generations, but it was only occupied during sunny vacations. Tru's head cocked. She could go up into the attic and become one of the lost. She could vanish in this house. Was that what was happening? Were some of these wealthy college kids simply dropping out of the pressure of their Ivy League lives? Hiding away in paradise?

She backed from the windows, turned, and went into the hall, unseen.

Tru passed all the way out the back door and onto the beach with a single thought in her head. It wasn't hard to be unseen, even in a house that was full. She had to jog in the chill morning air to catch up to Audrey's shivery figure.

"Oh my God!" Audrey threw up her hands "*There* you are. We thought you'd be on the beach!"

"I went back inside," Tru admitted. It was chilly today, after all. "You know about the girl?"

"I know." Audrey set her hands on her hips. Off behind her, Chantal and Blaine hurried back, Rod was already arriving. Their knot of people pulled together. Ava and Rupert. Win was the furthest away, and Tru stepped out between them all to greet him. She wasn't sure why she did this, just that she was — in fact — shaken, and she wanted to make sure he was okay.

His face was flushed with running. "Hey Tru. I didn't know where you were."

"Did you know a girl went missing last night?" She reached out to steady him by the shoulders.

He nodded back at her. "I know it's *creepy*. So, I'm relieved to see you."

Tru accepted the hug Win couldn't seem to hold back.

If she was shaken, he was nearly panicked. But then, how would she have felt if they'd all woken up, gone out back, and no one could find Audrey? Or Rod? Or... *Win*? She squeezed him back.

"We should go inside." Chantal wrung her small hands nervously.

Rod shook his head at them all, "No-no. Sad as this is—and that's *very*—the girl probably went into the sea and-"

"The water was *too cold* for swimming last night. It's been storming all across the island since we got here." Said Blaine's upper-crust French-Canadian accent. "You know what's going on, Roddy. The time is up. We're it."

"Stop freaking her out." Rod threw up his hands. "Trudy's only been here a few weeks."

She appreciated the concern, but Tru stepped in with a direct question to Blaine and Chantal. "You think it's The Bull."

"*Of course*, it's The Bull." Ava pushed by with Rupe beside her, caught hold of Audrey's hand on one side, and Chantal's on the other, and started everyone back toward the house. "Why do you think the beach is *empty*? The chill? With so many fire pits?"

Tru fell in beside Win, who threw his spare shirt around her shoulders in response to a sudden kick of wind. She marvelled, "You all *believe* in it."

With the sea starting to show signs of overcast and churn, Chantal looked back in her direction. "Live here for a while. *Then* tell me what *you* believe."

"Stop it." Audrey sounded exasperated and more than a little fearful. "It's just crummy weather. The police will find the missing girl. She's probably shacked up with some guy right now, blissfully unaware. And we'll be back in the rays after the storm."

But no one answered her.

The group seemed to tumble into the house on the crest of rough weather.

A beachcomber held the door open, the chef seemed to count noses. "Glad you're back, Misses and Misters." Said one of the men.

"Seriously?" Tru asked. She glanced back at the sound of the door locking behind them, but the maid scooted away without a backward glance. She went to close windows. And lock them. She drew the blinds.

Win's sudden squeeze of her hand was reassuring. Though he continued to look slightly fretful. "We'll stay in and have a movie night. With videogames. You said you loved videogames."

And she did. But even settling into the home-theatre room to *roast* rom-com tropes, eat snacks, cheer, and laugh, didn't remove it from Tru's head that something was wrong. She scurried to the washroom on bathroom break and discovered night was falling. She went to the back door and pulled the curtain aside to look at the leaping sea. *The island has changed.* "I smell it in the wind. I see it in the water."

"Miss?" One of the kitchen sous chefs came to her. "Glad you're here. I don't suppose you'd like to try a bit of satay and tell me if the peanut sauce is too hot? Ava and Audrey have delicate stomachs." She shut the curtain again as she spoke and then ushered Tru back toward the kitchen.

Everyone was on edge. She sat and even gamed, lost for hours, only to be pulled back to the notion of a missing girl—seventeen years of age, Caucasian, brown hair, and brown eyes—somewhere out in the pounding rain.

She went to bed with that thought and lay under the steady downpour until she could take no more. Even though she'd slept there was an ever-watchful part of her mind monitoring the sounds, the scents, and her sleeping experience of the world.

Finally, near to 4:30 AM, she woke at a thunderclap. Tru yawned, and padded to her en suite, then out again, having freshened up, to look out her window at the....

Figure in the downpour-darkened lane.

It stared back at her. From inside a rubber bull's mask.

Her heart jerked badly enough she saw stars for a moment.

Tru backed away from the windows and steadied herself.

After a few heartbeats, she turned, shut the door and went into the hall.

"Am I dreaming?" She gave her arm a few pinches. *No. That hurt.*

She went down the hallway and stood outside Audrey's bedroom door, hand poised to knock.

Okay, what am I doing, waking her at this hour? I should just.

Tru reversed to get some of the house stationary to write a note with, seeing as she'd left her phone in her bedside charger. She stopped because fresh night air blew into the hall. Immediately, Tru dropped into stillness. Some part of her quietened completely. In that place, she was no more than a stick of furniture in the long and broad hall. She would not react.

She stood and listened to a creak. And another.

How had he gotten in? She remembered the beachy crowds, the unlocked doors to the house, and her amusement as she patted her face dry. *Ah!* They'd been *fools*.

But the rest of her mind couldn't help but recall Ramona's words.

Well. My relative backed away, turned, and ran.

They fled through the entire night together, yet they didn't make it back till dawn.

And the whole way... it was behind him.

But what if... *the Great Bull* was *here*? Tru, somewhere in the stillness of her mind knew three things.

She'd seen it... turned, and run.

Dawn was 5:30 AM. She'd been on the beach for the dawn for *weeks* now.

Third thing—as the shadow of horns appeared on the floor down the hallway. Third thing. But her hold on stillness was becoming slippery. And her mind couldn't focus. She flashed back to standing in the window looking out at her friends thinking: *I could vanish in this house.*

Vanish. In the house.

Tru stepped backward down the hall, found the servant's stairwell, and scurried up it.

Her mind was racked as she moved between floors. Because she thought she could... could almost hear it. She paused, quiet and focused, on the dark and empty third floor. She glided room to room, the tiny creaks and cracks letting her know it was getting closer.

Tru stopped looking behind her.

Finally, she crept into the attic and ran across the great slab-wood expanse that was the footprint of the entire house. Huge wood rafters hung indifferently overhead, laced with zip-tied cabling that dropped down along posts that passed into different parts of the house. And she flashed back to movie night. Sunning on the beach. There wasn't much up here. No cover. Her bare footfalls left tracks in the dust. But would anyone ever find them?

She leapt through the staircase that led down. It was on the left of the house. Her heels cracked against the hardwood landing so that her weight threw her against the wall. But she shoved the exit door open and slammed it shut behind her back. Then leaned on it. She could hear him milling right on the other side.

And this was it.

Tru leaned, pinning it back, sweaty and panting as her eyes scanned the dark third floor.

Down. From here. The weight against the door let up. She could hear the clack of it backing away. Tru broke from the dark cubby at a full run, her night gown flying around her pumping limbs.

Racing in the hall, she could hear the crack of hooves, the splintering of the door.

How she got down the stairs to the second floor, Tru would never really remember. She touched so very few of the steps doing so. But her ankles hurt from leaping and landing. Her side had a stitch. And she was streaked with sweat as she sped up.

Tru ran the hall with its breaths on her back, and she hurtled straight over the top rail to the stairwell with her arms and legs flailing in air. She didn't feel the landing that sent her stumbling and falling to the floor. She tossed herself down the staircase toward the first floor and rolled, and behind her, the wood split, splintered, and bits of wainscot rained in a thunderclap.

The Great Bull bugled its frustration, momentarily caught.

Tru felt syrupy slow standing up again. Studiously *not* looking back. Somewhere above her, a girl... was it Audrey Dublin? Someone piped into darkness. "Hello? Hello?"

Tru knew she had to get the Bull outside.

She felt she was moving slowly.

She *tore* down the hall that led directly out back, only half-running.

She was half lifted off her feet, by the hot bow-wave at the front of the Great Bull. The doors blasted open amid rolling thunder, and she was thrown high and long out back of the house. In fact, she passed over the little wood steps, airborne, and spilled out on the sandy beach. The thing that passed over her head... was so massive she couldn't even... *think*. She couldn't *scream*. Black as smoking soot, and red as a hot coal, its forked hooves like stones, the Great Bull *was real*.

She felt herself begin to panic, her frantic breathing building into shrieks.

When she turned to run, she stopped cold, with her face inches from the wrought iron stake, the feeders tossed and blown aside.

She caught hold of it to stand, and Tru felt a calm overcome her.

She pulled herself up. Pulled out the stake as it was all she had.

Slowly. Tru turned on the headland.

It bucked and threw its burning horns in air. The rain obscured it. And fog leapt of its hot ember hide. It was a huge dark fairy, brought and buried here. For what else lived in mounds? The stillness descending on her seemed to answer *Fairies. And the dead.* Trapped here by the salt of the sea, its steps sizzling on the beach. The frustrated bull turned, its tremendous red eyes her way.

And it seemed... confused.

Tru understood that. How *could* it really see her? She was, more than she'd *ever* been, in the silent, still place inside, and — to its fairy eyes, burning bright — she must appear no different than the waves of the ancient sea in which her bloody feet were washed clean. Inside timelessness, Tru was cut from clear glass. From there, *she* watched *it*. And it seemed *slow*, smouldering in the rain. Finally, it turned its huge body — nearly a quarter of a mile down the beach — and she watched it blindly charge what it could no longer, truly see.

What did you do when you couldn't run anymore?

Tru raised the wrought iron stake. *You charged back.*

Her eyes narrowed as she tilted at the massive beast.

She shouted, as best she could remember.

Seven years I served thee,

the hills of glass surmounting.

A mantle white I brought thee.

And now you turn upon me?

The Great Bull made a startled bellow. Its massive hooves skidded in wet sand, and when it struck her, the stake bit into it. It drew blood that turned to smoke and mist. The wind of its charge also picked Tru up and threw her back, in a spray of sand.

It felt like... her toes slid along a tightrope between one world and the next. Stillness and this wet, rainy, painful place.

But Tru toppled onto a sandy beach, and then struggled to sit up.

It was only then that she became aware that it was raining.

And rain blurred the line between two worlds as well. The land, and the sea. She shook with cold.

Fire-orange on the horizon, nautical dawn lifted its blanket of star-dotted blackness and peeked at the world. Lights came on at Audrey's, and Tru could hear someone make discovery of the shattered kitchen door, bleat with dismay, and run deeper into the house, where—Tru could promise—it wouldn't be any better. Repairs though. Repairs sounded so nice and normal. She felt the stillness lifting as she sat, sea water up to her chest washing away her sweat in swells that passed over her head.

She sputtered, unsure how she'd not noticed *that, stillness* or *not.*

As the haze of grey set in, if she looked down along the sand, she could see the red hair of a young man who was, like her, collapsed half in the waves and half on the soaking shore.

But wrapped in a long white cloak.

Our final story is a delightful tale of Jar Fairies in a world that is part Oz, *part* Little Women. *The main character has traveled far to find help for her community. But there are miles to go and many things that can happen along the way. Penned by our Tinker Fairy of Books, it is an adventure not to be missed.*

FATEFUL ENCOUNTERS

Heidi Moone

PENNA EVERCLEAR COULD SEE THE clouds roiling in the distance, swallowing up the stars in the night sky, and those clouds weren't good news at all. She had a schedule, and a storm would ruin things.

But when you have a schedule, you keep to it until you can't. She proceeded to roll her beautiful, leaden glass jar down the hillside, mindful as she could be of the rocks and errant tree branches that jutted out, begging to ruin everything for Penna.

She had protected her jar as much as possible, having wrapped it in strips of cloth she'd taped on—though the tape was her enemy. It could stick to her as well, and since she was all of six inches tall, that could be as troublesome as a thunderstorm.

At the bottom of this latest hill, she decided to check the area for the best path forward. The journey she'd opted to take, for her kind, was perhaps foolhardy, but she was determined to be the one to succeed, and she'd come so far now. Penna checked the stars overhead, before they could be swallowed up by the churn of cloud barreling her way, and she was confident she was closer than ever.

Penna had lost so much time with the river. The river had been hard.

She'd lost Elki Freesky at the river.

Penna tried to redirect her thoughts away from that. Nothing was to be gained from the despair she'd felt, finding Elki's jar, with a crack in the side, and no sign of Elki.

No matter. No matter. She scouted, and in short order, she was rolling her jar over uneven ground, and into a bit of a clearing made by a bare rock and a fallen tree.

If the storm passed in time, there would be sunlight here, in this bit of glade in the forest at the bottom of the hill.

The clouds were swallowing up the crescent moon as she righted her jar, her hands shaking as she carefully took off the lid and peeled off the tape, preserving it as best she could by sticking it to the filthy wrappings and tossing the whole affair into the bottom of her jar.

Next, she had to get the jar upright. She could feel the chill breeze pick up as she took her spear and levered the jar upright, into a little nook created between rock and fallen tree branch.

She hoped it wouldn't block out too much sun.

She hoped the sun would actually come.

Then Penna crept up the side of the jar, dragging the lid behind her. Once inside, she was able to use the little handles, that had been fashioned for the lid's underside, to securely fasten it once more.

An important addition, for a jar fairy who'd never been meant to be able to open her own jar, she mused, sinking down and curling up to wait.

Then the rain fell, all at once. She'd been in time.

Penna watched the drops slither down her glass, until they ceased to be drops, and became more of a torrent that blurred, then obliterated the outside world.

She was so tired! But no rest could come, no true recovery, without the sun. At a low ebb, she began to examine herself, to see if there was any damage she might be able to mend for the time being.

She had already taped up her left leg, and Penna didn't dare to unwrap it to see the damage there. Her wings were listless, she could no longer fly, and it would be days of recovery if she hoped to do that again. She examined them nonetheless, silver-grey, translucent, lifeless.

Once, her wings had been so beautiful. Penna tried to clean them, but her hands were so dirty, she just kept making it worse.

Where were Elki's wings tonight? Where was Elki?

Where was Toko Goodbreeze, the third member of their party? Probably back with the others by now. Toko had taken her jar and turned back during the last storm. The ice had been thick, up higher in the mountains, the last of winter telling them how foolish they'd been.

Penna almost reluctantly reached up to where she'd bundled her hair. It felt stiff, filthy with muck, and it was bothersome. How she wanted to be clean of all this, suddenly!

She could always open the jar lid and let the rain pour in. It would be a sad bath, wouldn't it?

No water should get into her jar. Bad enough that there were mucky old cloths at the bottom, really. She felt underneath to where she'd taped on her precious payment, should she finish this journey in time.

Of course, it was still there, safe.

In the end, she straightened herself out in her wretchedness and made a little bed of the scraps of material, and waited for the rain to stop.

PENNA WAS AT LOW AWARENESS when the sun burst, brilliantly, into being all around her.

The air was suffused with light, and even through her jar, she could feel the quality of the air change. Water dripped off the lush, burgeoning bright green of spring, and she was so happy she could've shouted for joy, if she could shout at all.

However, ironically, now that the sun was here, the most Penna could do would be to sleep, to give herself the best possible chance at recharging. Her jar was well-positioned, she was as safe as she could make herself, and the storm had clearly passed. Penna closed her eyes, and her awareness passed for a time.

OF COURSE, THE SUN SHIFTING past her jar's position caused her to wake up again, in an instant. Penna was thrilled, she could feel how energized she was after having spent so much time in pure sunlight. How powerful she was again.

For a moment, she wanted to try her wings, and see if she could fly to scout.

But Penna had to be practical. She knew which way she needed to go, and she knew that she couldn't fly there. Couldn't risk losing track of her jar, her lifeline.

She quickly took the lid off, and then took out the wrappings, which she artfully put around and around her jar. She fussed with the tape, almost getting her right arm stuck, but at least she didn't get her wings stuck, which had almost happened her second morning out.

Then, she'd had the others to help her. Now, she was completely alone.

Once all that was done, she went and grabbed the jar's little makeshift handle. It was made of twine that her tribe had woven for just this purpose. She was stronger than she looked, and slowly, she set out, dragging her jar behind her.

If she'd been able to linger in the sun a couple of days, she might be able to fly with her jar, but now, a trudge was the most she could manage. Soon, she came to another hill, and she began rolling the jar up, pausing every now and again to rest when the sun fell on her.

Maybe another hour with the jar would be a good idea? But the sun was already starting to descend in the sky. Penna wouldn't have another hour.

She waded through dead tree needles and forest rot, turning to mulch in the warming of spring. Penna checked her taped leg regularly, because she felt certain that it would be the greatest risk to her success right now.

She stopped once, when she saw a squirrel. It looked at her curiously, but in the end, it neither challenged her nor ran from her. She was grateful for that. She didn't need a squirrel fight right now.

As the sun dipped lower, Penna came out of the woodline, unexpectedly, and found an entire meadow.

Ah, if only she'd found this before the storm had come in, overnight! She would've had so much more sunlight today!

Penna found a burbling brook, and took some time, precious time, to at least clean herself and her jar a little. It wasn't vanity. She needed her jar to be as clean as possible, even with everything she was putting it through.

Along the way, she inspected it for any cracks or other damage. There were a couple of minor chips in the bottom, but nothing too alarming. Every fairy's jar had a chip or two in it, after a while. When she was done, Penna actually hugged her jar, her very own jar, and took comfort in it before wrapping it up again and setting out.

She would, once again, walk through the night until she could go no further. She would walk until she found a good place for the coming day.

THE WINGS WERE ALMOST SILENT, but Penna's hearing was exceptional.

The owl still almost had her, talons sharp and grasping. She made not a sound, because there was no sound she could make, but the little fairy scrambled, looking for anything in the new copse of trees between her and her destination.

The owl was hungry, and wouldn't realize what a poor meal a small jar fairy like her might make.

Penna wasn't unfamiliar with predators. All the fairies who had begun this quest knew the risks, and had prepared themselves. She took her spear and waited for the bird to come around.

Owls. As fantastically gifted as hunters was how idiotic they were as reasoners. When the bird came for her again, she jabbed it in the side of the leg, but a talon caught her and started to bring her into the dark sky.

It was everything Penna could do to stay calm as she twisted and jabbed at the bird again. The talon tightened on her legs, but then she was falling, free.

Despite the waste of her precious energy, Penna spread her damaged wings and managed a sort of controlled fall, but the owl had already flown her so far from her jar, and in the dark, which way had they flown?

First, she needed to not have the owl attack her again, but her small defense had apparently given the owl enough to think about that it didn't return a third time.

Then, she took stock of the trees. She was further, she thought, than she had been before the attack. She would need to go back to find her precious jar. The jar that she needed to stay alive. The jar with the payment secured inside of it.

To lose the jar was to lose everything.

Penna flew, flew out of the copse altogether, and managed to orient. She landed and crept back to where her jar was, wings drooping as she finally came within sight of it.

She hugged her jar, shaken with relief and weakness. Her strength was much diminished as she leaned on the jar, and it was with a desperate reluctance that she took up the twine and began to drag it through the remainder of the trees.

She had also lost her spear, but fortunately, she still had two left in the jar.

DAWN CAME, AND IT FOUND Penna already in her jar, which was not far from a babbling brook.

The latest obstacle, but also a hope for Penna. Because according to the directions she had, the road she was looking for was close to a brook, much like this brook.

As the colors bled into the sky and the world around her, Penna examined the injuries from the owl's talons.

Her torso, she bandaged as best she could, with slivers of cloth she'd tried to wash clean in the brook. It wasn't very practical, but there wasn't a lot to be done at this point.

Her leg, her poor left leg, seemed weaker than ever, and she rubbed it anxiously. There was nothing she could do for it, except to keep going. Elki would've kept going.

Had Elki lain there, not far from her jar, hoping that Penna would search and find her? Had she given up on the other fairy too soon? Penna hugged herself as the jar began to warm, and her system began to relax in spite of her wandering mind.

She should've stayed and looked for Elki. Penna knew Elki would never have left her behind. That's who Elki was, and she'd only come on this journey because Penna had been so determined to go.

She'd left someone that loyal behind, and now there was nothing to be done.

As she started to wind down, Penna watched a tiny worm wriggle out of the earth, sliding along a blade of grass, on some unknowable quest.

Surely that was a sign, as she too was a creature thrust into a strange new world, trying to make her way in this place, so beautiful and yet hostile. She pressed her hand against her jar, feeling a bond between the two of them.

As she passed from consciousness, soaking up the sun's rays in her jar, Penna fortunately missed a passing robin hopping by and devouring that tiny worm.

WHEN PENNA AWAKENED, IT WAS startling to find she was being watched.

The fox, a lavender creature with an intelligent eye, had lain down to keep an eye on her jar. Penna wasn't quite sure what to make of the large, dangerous creature, but she didn't have a lot of fight in her, even if she was feeling much better after a day in her jar.

Had the fox tried to get in? She looked at the glass all around, but saw no scratches or new chips. The lid was still securely on, for which she was grateful.

Sitting back down, she looked at the fox, who didn't seem in a hurry to move along. Drat.

Well, she still had two spears. She untaped one from the side of her jar, and confirmed it had a solid point and would function as both a weapon and a new walking stick for her. Part of Penna was confident the fox would tire of her and leave sometime in the night, but the moon was getting fatter, and she was worried she would miss the creature she hoped to make contact with.

That fateful meeting could only happen in the next day or two, or not at all, as far as Penna was concerned. It would be months, possibly, before the next encounter. And what could she do, as hurt as she'd become, in the interim?

How long did her village have, if she wasn't successful?

Finally, she felt like she couldn't wait any longer. She lifted up and unscrewed her jar lid, and cautiously crept out of the protection of her most precious possession, dragging her spear and her rags with her.

The fox cocked its head, but didn't immediately attack.

Wasting no time, Penna started to wrap up the jar, the tape feeling weaker than ever. At this rate, it wouldn't last the trip back, putting her little jar in more peril.

No matter. She would worry about that when it came time. Perhaps she could take some of her twine and knot it up somehow to bind the rags. Or she could find more tape.

The fox sat upright, head still cocked.

If Penna could speak, she would've yelled at the fox, perhaps, or tried to scare it off. As it was, she took her small spear and banged it against the lid of her jar. Carefully, because she didn't want to damage it! But it made a slight, tinny clanging noise, and the fox finally loped off, into the gathering gloom.

Penna thought the world might have too many predators in it.

Now, the brook. She could try crossing it, it was much smaller than the river, but the river crossing had needed two fairies, and she was only one now.

She could follow it, and see if it brought her to a road. But upstream, or downstream?

Was there any way around it? Penna looked up, and she fluttered her wings experimentally.

It would be a lot of energy, to fly so high. Her strength would be at a low ebb for the rest of the night.

But how much energy would she waste if she went the wrong way? With everything that was at stake, Penna couldn't imagine not taking this one chance.

Her wings began to glow, orange and yellow, like the life-sustaining sun, and she focused on having them lift her up, up into the air.

Yes, she was wobbly, as her feet left the ground. Penna couldn't even take her new spear, she needed to be as light as possible for this to work, but soon, she was several feet high, and then she could see in the light of the setting sun, a road, and even a little wooden bridge, upstream of the brook.

Penna let her wings still, and fell, then caught herself on the air, and then fell again, to conserve as much of her strength as she could. Even so, she hit the ground harder than she'd like, and her left leg twinged a little as a result.

All things considered? Worth the risk. Penna picked up her spear, looked around to be sure there was no fox, and then set off to follow the brook upstream to the road she'd sacrificed so much to reach.

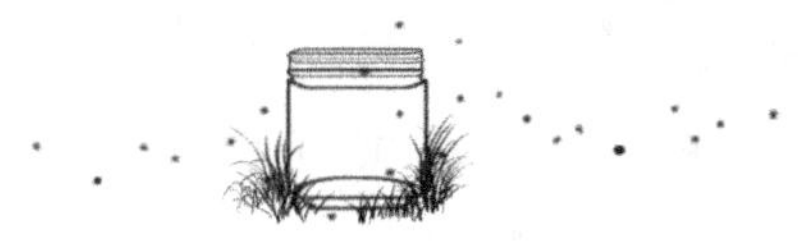

BY THE TIME SHE REACHED the road, Penna was almost ready to unpack her jar and set it up to wait for sunrise. Flying had taken so much out of her, and all of her ached, really. Her wings, unused to exertion, twitched and spasmed every now and again. Her left leg ached and twice, if she hadn't had the spear, she would've collapsed to the ground.

Penna was ready to accept this might be a one-way journey, but she would not fail in what she'd set out to do.

Unless she was simply too late, and had missed the encounter entirely.

The road was smooth, and hard, and Penna was faced with a new problem. How could she possibly drag her poor jar along such a surface? This was not loamy earth or a grassy field. This was dangerous.

Reluctantly, she trudged along the side of the road, almost in a bit of a ditch. If she needed to pull her jar up onto the road, she really might have to surrender to the inevitable and set up for the morning sun.

Then she came to the bridge, the tiny little wooden thing, and Penna tried not to be too excited. She could see symbols carved into this bridge, which was what she'd been expecting.

Out of a small pocket, she pulled a drawing made by the leader of their fairy tribe.

She saw two dots, a swirl like a snake, and then a triangle. This was the correct bridge, the one she'd needed to find.

If Penna had it in her, she might've knelt and wept. Instead, she gingerly dragged her jar onto the wooden slats, careful to hop over the small spaces between boards. None of them were big enough for her to fall through, but one of her feet could possibly get stuck, and that wouldn't be helpful at all.

It was interesting, that the road was wide, but the bridge was narrow. If anyone came along of a particular size, Penna knew they would not be able to pass side-by-side.

In the middle of the night, fortunately, she had the place to herself, and Penna made the crossing quickly. She crept back into the undergrowth next to the road, and then she actually rested for a minute, the enormity of it all hitting her.

She was actually close to the end of it now. She just had to reach the market, and find the tinkerer.

So, why was she hiding in the undergrowth? Penna squared her shoulders, looked at her jar, and nodded. She would do this, all on her own, because it had to be done.

NEVER HAD PENNA BEEN SO happy to see the first signs of dawn staining the sky. She found a corner in the road, and trekked away from it, into a field dazzling with budding wildflowers. Spring was in a hurry, which was beautiful, but dangerous.

Penna didn't want to have to deal with rivers of mud on the way back.

But, that was assuming going back was even an option. She crept into her jar, with the motley scraps of cloth already in the bottom, and prepared for the first rays of dawn to come and restore her.

As the beautiful, life-giving warmth crept over her, Penna's consciousness slipped away, but she was sure she saw a glimpse of a familiar, lavender-furred face settling in to watch her with patience and curiosity.

THE WORLD WAS ROCKING, GENTLY back and forth, as Penna's awareness returned.

What could possibly be happening? She looked around, and then felt quiet panic as she realized she was nowhere sensible.

There was no field of ambitious wildflowers. No gentle breeze making the plants dance, while running up against the impervious curve of glass that was her jar.

The sun was still there, and in fact, she dangled from the twine affixed to her jar's lid, drinking it in. Whatever had happened to her, someone had at least done her this kindness. As she sat in her jar, unexpectedly captive to whatever circumstance had been thrust upon her, she tried not to panic.

Was she even going in the right direction down the road? What had happened to her?

Penna faced a daunting choice.

She could unscrew the jar's lid, and she would fall free. But from the height she was above the road, dangling from an iron outcropping of some sort, Penna was sure her jar wouldn't survive the fall. And even then, what was a jar fairy with no lid?

It was an impossible choice. She could be free, but only for one final day, and then, she'd be done for.

Would it be enough? That depended on which way she was travelling right now.

Penna turned, and from between slats of wood, she saw a lavender fox face looking at her through a window. The little creature cocked its head and then made a yipping noise, and vanished.

How could that be a good thing? Penna felt the lurching vehicle she was on start to slow, and eventually it lumbered to a stop, right in the road.

"Now, now, let's have a look at you," a voice said, in a heavy sort of accent. Penna knew the words, however. She pressed her grimy little hands to the glass of her jar and looked up as a figure appeared from the direction of the front of the vehicle.

The speaker was short and squat, and unfolded itself like a child's puzzle, until legs and arms appeared. She could see gears moving underneath layers of well-worn clothing, and two bright green eyes, like gems, adjusted themselves slightly in a cheerful clockwork face to look at her. The figure was cast in bronzes, mostly, with some replacement parts in brassiest brass or a dull, tarnished sort of silver dotted here and there.

The silver extended to its hair, which was made of tightly coiled silver springs, though they had no tarnish in them.

The speaker's voice ground like a music box, but was intelligible otherwise, as the clockwork person stepped up.

"Little jar fairy, my fox found you in a field this morning, and came to tell me all about you," the voice said. "I left you dangling in the sun by your clever twine, and I told her to come and let me know when you stirred. You've rested in the sun all day, and so you must have been so tired."

Penna, trembling, could only cross her hands over her heart and bow. She had no voice to respond with.

"Such a shy little fairy. Jar fairies are famous for their beautiful voices and singing, but perhaps it is not so with you?"

She shook her head.

"I have been asked, by someone I much admire, to collect up any jar fairies I might come across, and bring them along, and so have I done this. You are clearly on a journey, and I know I did not ask your permission. After I have taken you to the Night Market at the Crossroads, someone can carry you onward, to make up for this delay," the clockwork person offered.

Penna didn't believe such a thing. Nothing happened in this world without payment. The jar fairies had learned this the hard way, and it was a lesson they took to heart. No gift without sacrifice. No boon without cost.

She looked back up at her abductor, realization dawning in her, however.

The Night Market at the Crossroads was her final destination. Could it be, that this untoward creature had done her a favor, however inadvertently?

She nodded her head. No matter what happened after they arrived, nothing would thwart her from finding the tinkerer in the Night Market and offering payment for a most important service.

"So strange, I had hoped to hear the most enchanting sound! But if it is not to be, then it must be what it is." The clockwork being patted its own chest, and bowed. "I am Fatime, I travel back and forth, living a restless life and trading in favors."

That sounded anything but promising.

"I will take you to the front of my little home on wheels," Fatime said, and in short order, Penna dangled from a hook meant for a lamp, with a clear view of the road ahead, and two clockwork beasts who drew the covered wagon along.

All sorts of things hung from the wagon, all of them showing signs of good use. Inside a window, she could just peek and see things swaying back and forth from hooks. None of them seemed to be jar fairies, or anything else living, for that matter. The lavender fox crept out through a hole and curled up on the seat beside Fatime.

"Such a curious creature, the fox. She comes and goes as she pleases, but she always has interesting things in mind," Fatime explained. "You know, she it was who found me, and not the other way around. I have suspicions about her, but she is too charming to fret about it much."

The fox, for her part, apparently wasn't worried about much at all, other than sleeping.

Not having to walk, and drag her jar, meant that Penna could actually look around at the world as the color began to leech out of it. Soon, it would be dark, and only the light of the one remaining lantern would guide them.

Penna saw more trees along the road now, and the road was wider, if that was even possible. They went over two bridges in the time it took to grow dark, and she realized it would've been a much farther journey for her than she'd anticipated.

Each of the bridges held the same markings. Who knew, then, if she'd found the bridge she'd been instructed to look for, or just a random bridge with the right markings on it?

Penna still had the option of unscrewing the lid from the inside once she got to the Night Market, and she would have a much better chance of finding the tinkerer and making her request.

She smoothed down her jar lovingly. Penna could admit, she didn't want to lose it. Her entire life had been spent in this little space, resting comfortably while the sun sustained her.

"Do you make the music, jar fairy who does not speak or sing?"

Penna looked at Fatime, who was looking at her with one eye, while the other remained on the road.

She nodded, and then made motions. She could play a harp, and she could play a zither as well. Once, she had been a great musician, until her tribe had traded their instruments for more important things.

"I have a little treasure for you then. I will trade it to you to play, for music while we go," Fatime offered, and Penna nodded. This was a trade she would accept.

And Fatime brought the wagon to a stop once more, and went into the little wagon house, emerging with a tiny harp. The strings were, miraculously, intact, though the beautiful paints had almost worn completely away.

"Don't stab me with your poison spear," Fatime cautioned. "I may be a clockwork woman, but I know your poisons can still hurt the likes of me, jar fairy."

Penna shook her head. Her tiny spears were not poisonous. She was no elf, roaming in raucous bands with their tiny poison containers, ready to dip their spears and arrows into whatever concoction they needed in a given moment.

She received the harp, and ran her hands across it reverently. Certainly, never hers, but some other jar fairy had once held this, had once loved it. Although it had been many seasons, Penna's fingers were certain as she tuned the harp, and then began to play.

Even without her voice, her body strained as though it would sing, and the music at once was mournful and sad, playing the tune of all Penna knew she had lost.

"The night would cry, if it could," Fatime said after a time. "Your story is a sad one then, jar fairy."

Penna couldn't even offer a small gift of her name, but eventually, she began to play different music, livelier, and just as she finished up a bit of a reel, she noticed that there was light in the world beyond the fattening moon overhead and the lamp to their right.

Could it be?

She leaned forward, having gently laid the harp to one side.

"It has been a good exchange, this gift," Fatime murmured. While Penna waited, wondering what could happen next, the most glorious sight unfolded.

DESPITE HER TASTE FOR ADVENTURE, Penna had never been to a Night Market, she had only heard the stories, across the seasons. She watched as traffic began to come and go with them, as they caught up to other wagons, and carts, and even a sledge that floated in mid-air through some unseen mechanism.

Creatures of all types abounded. She watched a luminous stick figure walking with a bundle on its back that pulsed slightly, and a gaggle of geese were ushered along by a girl whose feet were also geese feet, though the rest of her looked like an ordinary human girl. She grinned at the jar fairy as she looked up.

Wonder after wonder unfolded, and then the booths started to crop up.

On the outskirts were people selling concoctions, a juggler, and some sort of stage had been set up, gathering a crowd. Fatime had no time for any of this, and she seemed to know where she was going.

Penna could admit, she had little idea how she could've navigated all this. She couldn't ask for directions without a voice. All the fairies had their own hand-language that they had taught one another once their voices had been sold, but it wasn't the same as being able to use speech.

She could, with difficulty, write something large enough for people to read. But she would need a pen and something to write on.

Finally, the din of the Night Market caused her to start to panic a little, and she covered her ears with her hands.

"This is a busy night, jar fairy," Fatime said. "We are almost there."

They had reached what must've been the heart of the market, and Fatime took a side-route, and ended up in front of a rather elaborate booth.

"This is Tinker Moxie, and she has made a request for any jar fairies to be brought to her," Fatime said. "I am not unkind, but I confess, a favor for a tinkerer is a valuable thing when one is made of gears."

Penna nodded. She could fully appreciate that.

But she was confused. The tinkerer she had been told to find in the Night Market was Tinker Jobe. He'd been described to her as stern and exacting, but a good, steady hand, and now there was a second tinkerer?

How to escape from one to the other? Penna felt more intimidated than ever. And this Moxie had made it a goal to actually collect jar fairies? Why?

With no say in her fate for the moment, she didn't try to unscrew her jar lid as Fatime took her off the hook and brought her to the counter of the booth Moxie kept. There was a door to one side, and Penna realized this was a permanent sort of building.

"Hey there, Flit, is your master in?"

Fatime spoke to a wisp of a child, a literal wisp, who promptly bowed and then walked through a wall covered with gears, levers, and small gadgets.

"What you got there, Fatime?"

The voice came, not from the booth, but from the street. Fatime straightened and looked, and so did Penna, and they both saw a tall, thin man made of wood standing there.

His hair was moss, and he wore bark clothing in a patchwork of colors. His frown seemed permanently etched into his face, and perhaps it was a carved face, at that. Penna had seen wooden folk before, up in the mountains. They tended to be solitary.

If you didn't trouble them, they wouldn't trouble you. Once, one of them had been a friend to the jar fairies, and had even ventured down to the Night Market, once or twice, to barter for them.

This wood man's feet were bare, more root-like than anything else. The wooden folk liked to be close to the earth. Some of them became lucky enough to turn back into trees, and this was what had happened to Twig, their friend, one fine spring.

"Barque, I'm conducting business," Fatime said in a patient voice.

Perhaps this wood man might be inclined to help her find Tinker Jobe? Penna was anxious. A strange tinkerer could have any intention at all, and how likely was she to recommend a rival?

It was all suddenly out of control.

You're bringin' one of them fairies to her, she doesn't need all the fairies," Barque said. "I can give you better for that li'l thing than Moxie will, mark my words."

"Duly marked, Barque," Fatime said, turning to face him as she leaned on the booth counter. "What's your coin for this transaction?"

"I got oil, I got gears, I can even give you a straw of silver," he nodded.

Penna saw Fatime's silver-bronze eyebrows rise.

"You would trade a genuine silver straw for a jar fairy?"

Was it Penna's imagination, or did Barque manage to look even more sour?

"Said it," he said. "And they're a passing valuable asset right now in the Night Market. It's a fair exchange."

"All those things are fine," Fatime mused. "But nothing's as valuable as the expertise of a first-rate tinkerer, and Tinker Moxie and her sisters are the only ones at this Night Market, nowadays."

Penna looked at her in shock.

This was horrible news. What had happened to Tinker Jobe?

"I'm sure we can find something worth more than she'll offer you," he said, sounding very confident. "Come over to my booth, and we can talk."

"Barque, I still don't know this sudden fascination with jar fairies, but go away." A strong, feminine voice spoke up, and Penna turned in her jar to see a most amazing sight.

A woman stood there, a human woman, Penna thought, from her limited experience. She had a hat on, and no hair that Penna could speak of, apart from frosted blonde eyebrows. One of those was half-singed off, from the looks of it.

She wore overalls and a tight grey shirt that might've been another color once, and over that, a sort of coat or smock with burns all up the sleeves. One pair of goggles rested on her forehead, and another around her neck.

Penna hadn't seen many humans in a long, long time. She blinked at this one, wondering who she should even be rooting for. The ominous wooden man, or the obviously human woman?

"Anyone's got the right to do business in the market," the wooden man said, decidedly not going anywhere.

None of this felt good or right to Penna, who decided she might as well choose now to make a break for it. Surely they were wrong. Tinker Jobe had to be somewhere in this place. She began to reach up and unscrew her jar lid.

"Thank-you for bringing her to me," Tinker Moxie said to Fatime. "I've been expecting a jar fairy for a little while now. I will offer a night's services for maintenance, and also parts for your arm will be greatly discounted when they arrive."

"Fair trade," Fatime nodded. "Thought I might pay full and have you look at my nightgear's left front hoof."

"I can look for you," Moxie nodded. "Thrown in as a courtesy."

They were both ignoring Barque now, who grumbled as he turned and left.

Penna had the jar almost unscrewed when a fog enveloped her jar, and Flit's ghostly hands twisted the lid back on.

The wisp of a girl didn't speak, and just shook her head, no.

If Penna could've yelled at her, she would've, but then, alarmingly, her jar was laid on the booth counter, and Moxie swept it up.

"Hello, little jar fairy," she said, her eyes had wrinkles next to them so close-up, and she had freckles on her nose. "It's a pleasure to finally meet you. I think your name is Penna, yes?"

Penna held her breath, because how was that possible?

"Is that her name?" Fatime sounded pleased. "Penna. Thank-you for that."

"Well, I can't be sure, are you Penna?" Moxie asked, and Penna, reluctantly, nodded. She turned back to where Fatime stood, and half-bowed from her torso.

"She has been good company. That harp has been my gift to her, and an apology for waylaying her on her own journey," Fatime explained. "However, as you know her name, perhaps this has been her destination the entire time?"

"It has," Moxie said, smiling as Penna spun to look back at her. "Though I rather think she was looking for my father, Tinker Jobe."

And all was explained. Penna nodded, her confusion clearing up in an instant.

Humans had children, and this was Jobe's child. She would keep the promises Jobe had made, so many seasons ago.

As she nodded again, a little frantically now, Moxie handed the jar to Flit, who was barely solid enough to hang onto the twine.

"Take the door, Flit, and put her back with the others," she said. "I need to finish my business with Fatime."

"Good-bye for now, tiny Penna," Fatime said, sounding sad. "I believe we may adventure together again, so, I shall rather say until then."

That was the last Penna saw of her accidental rescuer and the lavender fox.

Flit brought her back into a work area, and lugged her to a shelf, where Penna was shocked to see a sight she couldn't have imagined before now.

No less than a dozen different jar fairies were there, some in jars, some outside. All of them seemed to be unconscious, and some of them were in a decided state of disrepair!

She gasped in horror as she saw, of all fairies, Toko Goodbreeze, asleep in her very own jar in front of a great light. And on the table her jar now rested on was Elki Freesky, who looked like she might not be alive any longer.

This couldn't stand! Having suddenly recovered her friends, Penna wouldn't allow some tinkerer to do them harm, and she immediately set to unscrewing her jar lid once the wispy girl had vanished further into the interior of the workroom.

Furiously, Penna undid her jar's lid, and then she took a spear and left the dubious safety of her home, making her way toward poor Elki.

Elki's wings were gone, and part of her face was a ruin. When Penna put her hands on her oldest friend's arm, there was no sign of life, no warmth at all.

Penna leaned over the friend she never thought she'd see again, and gasped with the pain of it all.

"Penna, Penna, it's going to be all right."

She bared her little teeth at the sound of the tinkerer's voice, and Penna snatched up her little spear, brandishing it as the tall human woman stepped forward with a heavy glove on.

She took to the air with very little grace, but she had managed to surprise Moxie, who stepped back and looked thoughtful.

"And you can still fly, I can see why they believed in you," the tinkerer said, and she reached across her bench and took a small net.

Penna would *never* be caught in a net again! She flew backward, only to be startled by an origami cat who was sleeping high on a shelf.

And in that moment, a gentle hand grabbed her, being uncommonly careful about her wings. Tinker Moxie took the spear from Penna, and she gently took a pin, pressing it into a spot between Penna's two wings.

"Rest, Penna, I'll explain everything when you wake up."

But Penna was already unconscious.

"PENNA EVERCLEAR, BRAVE AS BRAVE, and knows no fear, has the hearts of her friends held dear, awake, awake, for me."

Penna liked the sound of that. It sounded like Elki Freesky's voice, from long, long before.

She was bathed in light. It lifted her up and held her like liquid gold, and as the music from a harp played on, Penna opened eyes that, if she could've seen herself, would've been golden like the sun itself, for the first time in years.

The first thing she knew was that she was clean. Clean as she hadn't been in ever so long, right down to her hair. She held out a hand, turned golden in the light, and saw no scars or scrapes, just...her.

Then she saw her jar. It was one of the jars held up near a light, a light that felt so much like the sun to her. Penna inhaled the light, and realized she could feel the energy sizzling in her wings.

She sat up, flexing them, and watching the power course through them, up and down. They were the colors of the sun, orange and gold, and paler yellows bleeding almost to white, and Penna just wanted to cry, because she hadn't remembered how beautiful they could be.

Who would want to take so much time to do such a thing? No one gave to a jar fairy. People only took from Penna and her kind, ever since they had escaped, so long ago.

Freedom was the best thing, but you paid for it.

"Penna." She hadn't imagined it. That was, somehow, Elki's voice. Penna turned, and took in her oldest friend in all her former glory.

Elki's eyes were blue, dark blue like the sky just after sunset, with a tinge of purple, pink, and green to it. Her wings were much the same, and her hair was darker still, a blue-black of midnight.

"Penna, I knew you, of all of us, would come and find the tinkerer," she said, grinning in a blistering way, a grin to even put sunlight to shame. "Did you walk all the way?"

She lifted her hands and signed that she had, in fact, ridden once she had been picked up, after finding the road and a bridge.

"Oh, you followed the road and everything! You would have made it," Toko Goodbreeze, whose eyes were aqua and whose hair was like seafoam, nodded as she appeared from around a corner, talking with another fairy. From the looks of it, another jar fairy, but one Penna had never seen before in all her years.

"Axa Sweetmist, this is the one we spoke of, the brave Penna Everclear."

Axa Sweetmist, had flashing silver eyes, to match her wings, which also had white and pale purple lights. Her hair seemed indeed to almost be made of mist as she bowed to Penna, who was now leaning on the edge of her very own glass jar, which had even had small repairs made to it. She could barely make out the epoxy fixes on her tiny chips.

Toko had her voice as well. What wonder was this?

"I've heard songs about you, Penna, it's a pleasure to meet another fairy from the mountain tribe," Axa nodded. "We are a delegation from the marshes."

"Aha, I thought I heard you all talking." Tinker Moxie stepped into the room, with smoke coming off a pair of heavy gloves she took off, and threw in a metal bucket. Behind her, Flit poured water from a teacup onto the gloves.

"She's awake," Elki said, unnecessarily.

Penna was distracted by the perfection of her left leg, now free of tape. Someone had repaired her, all of her. She moved the leg, and it was flawless. All her mechanisms had been repaired.

She checked her internal gauge, and found she was almost perfectly charged up with solar energy as well. Was it the power of the mysterious light?

"Penna, I'm Tinker Moxie, and once, my father dealt with you in a manner I've long considered unfair," Moxie said. "Come, let's take our refreshments while I tell you about what I know."

She nodded, and gently Moxie took Penna's jar from the vicinity of the light, and unscrewed the lid for her.

Penna stepped out, and Toko waited there with a gossamer gown that was mint green. It wasn't lost on Penna, either, that her jar was empty of dirty old rags, that it had been meticulously cleaned.

And that the taped-up payment in the bottom of the jar had been missing.

She signed to Toko, asking if the tinkerer would help them, and Toko hugged Penna, as hard as she could.

"Open your mouth, Penna, and let's see if you have the right voice back," Toko asked her, and Penna felt her face get hot like the sun was on it, as she closed her eyes.

"But my voice can't be back," she said, and then gasped, because indeed, it was there.

"Oh my goodness," she said, her hands fluttering to her neck. "But how?"

"My father took your voices as payment, he took your instruments, and this time, you had even brought wings to him," Moxie said as she served them all a drop of the essential oil that jar fairies loved, in cups that they could actually hold in their hands.

"But my father didn't sell any of these things," Moxie continued, sitting down with a strange-smelling beverage that seemed to be an unappealing brown, like mud-water. "We found these, and many other treasures, when we inherited his booth here in the Night Market."

"Once, your father would travel far and wide," Elki said, sporting a pale orange dress that looked good against her blueness. "We found him in that way, but knew that if we didn't meet up with him at the right time in the right season, we would be set for disappointment."

"Father did like to disappoint," Moxie said, a shadow of sadness passing across her face, like a cloud over the sun. "But there are five of us Tinker girls now, and while we all like to take a turn at wandering, there's always one of us at the Night Market, whatever the season."

Flit smirked a little as she passed through the area, barely substantial at the moment.

"Flit here likes my older sister Trixie best, don't you, wispy-wisp?"

Unabashedly, the incorporeal girl nodded.

"But we all agreed, when we appreciated what our father had done, that we were fortunate enough to try and make some things right," Moxie explained. "And so, when jar fairies started to come in from one cluster or another, we started matching up wings, and voices, and instruments, and anything else that had been sacrificed along the way, to put things back."

"But how do we pay for help now?" Penna asked, and Moxie nodded.

"In the Night Market, you don't have to sell bits of you," she explained. "Jar fairies have beautiful voices, and are brave, and lovely to behold. You can store up enough light to last for days, if you're given the chance, and you haven't stripped your wings of the cells that will hold so much energy. You can work, and earn the things you need without giving up more than your time."

"We jar fairies have enough time," Toko said, and Elki nodded.

Penna wasn't sure. Yes, they had been restored, they were clean, and beautiful, and whole. But there were so many jar fairies back home who were anything but.

"I am going to, once my baby sister Mitzi gets back, come with you to find your home in the mountains," the tinkerer continued. "Roxy, my twin, will be here in three nights with a wagon we can take."

"Jinx, another sister, has already taken a wagon back to the marshlands to help us," Axa explained. "My sisters and I decided we will work here, in the Night Market, and pay them back for their kindness to us."

"We've helped almost a dozen of the jar fairy tribes," Moxie said with obvious pride. "And I've long waited for someone from the mountains to come, so we could finally find you and help you, too."

"Penna, one of us can lead them back," Elki said, entwining her arm in Penna's, "and the others can stay here and take jobs as the other fairies do. We can go on adventures like we talked about, and see many things that the mountains don't have."

"Or," Toko noted, "we can go home with them, and see if someone else wants to have adventures."

"I have my voice back," Penna said, putting her head against Elki's. "I still don't know...how did you all come to be here? How did you survive?"

Elki quaffed the last of her little cup of oil and laughed, her face whole and beautiful.

"For my part, I was found by Toko, who had a change of heart, and then we were found by a scarecrow, but that's a long story, isn't it?"

"I'm making a song of it," Toko smiled, and Penna shivered, wondering how much work she could do to find a good lacquer for the harp Fatime had given her.

"You can sing it all to me, before we decide who will go back and save our village," she decided. "For my part, I'm not afraid of an adventure."

"That's the spirit," Moxie's eyes sparkled with delight, as a bell rang somewhere. "Ah, a customer!" She leapt to her feet. "Ladies, please feel free to continue on without me."

Penna turned and hugged Elki.

"I'm sorry I left you," she said. "I found your jar, and I thought...I thought the worst had happened."

"I didn't even find your jar," Elki murmured back, smoothing back Penna's unruly curls. "But I knew nothing would stop you, the bravest jar fairy in the mountains."

Penna didn't think that was very accurate, looking back on her own story. But perhaps, after Toko made a song out of it, she'd feel differently about the entire thing.

Sometimes that's how adventures worked.

ABOUT THE AUTHORS

TRACY **E**IRE has been a professional writer for almost a decade writing to a variety of needs, from the magazine Beautiful Bizarre, to collaborations with artists like Jenny Boot. In the mid-2000s, she started her art career and fiction publications. An oil painter with interest in watercolour painting, she was creatively influenced by her childhood home of Newfoundland. The wildness, mysticism, and kindness of this Northern island home just a step out of time, translated into optimism and depictions of light in art. The stamp of those wild climes and pagan survivals became strong impulses in her writing. They can be seen from her rich cast of mystical characters, to the haunting moments we all experience to one side of the flow of normal life, captured in her books. A seasoned writer, she's neurodiverse. Overcoming her disabilities with grit and flexibility creates a highly individual point of view in her work.

Please visit her at <u>tracyeire.site</u>

EMBER **F**ANE has hung a sign above her stories that says, "Read at your own risk." While her humorous side often sparkles, not even she knows what haunted chasm or labyrinthine alley her stories might twist along. Anywhere from the black between the stars through fifty shades of fae, she tells stories of many different hues under the science fiction and fantasy umbrella.

She loves to hear from her readers via emberfane@gmail.com

ELIZABETH KNOLLSTON has always been an avid reader of science fiction and fantasy. Now she works on turning her vivid imagination of alien worlds, long lost secrets of the universe, mystical realms and the obligatory dragon into stories of her own. Often blending religious questions and an abiding love for archeology into the driving forces behind her worlds. When not daydreaming about why the local pet store doesn't carry baby dragons, or being a part of a manned mission to Mars, Elizabeth teaches therapeutic riding, spends time with her dog, works in the garden, and loves giving back to the community.

HEIDI MOONE writes things. She says, "I've started to publish some of these things to share them with others. I like writing stories about fantastic places and the magic in the everyday world. I've been reading, and writing, from an early age, and I come from a tradition of oral storytellers, in rural Newfoundland. I love the written word, and it's my favorite medium to communicate my ideas to anyone looking for a new world to explore, and new people to meet along the way."

Please visit her at **heidimoone.com**

KARLI STITES is a tech nerd by day (and also by night), so she did the only thing she could when faced with an overload of creativity that had nowhere to go: she started writing sci-fi and fantasy novels. Karli published the first book in her debut series, Edge of Destruction, in 2019 and the space opera trilogy will be completed in 2021. A lover of all things fantasy and mythological, Karli was excited to dive into the world of dragons and intends to expand her dragonverse further in the future.

Check out her website at karlistitesauthor.com to join her newsletter and keep an eye on upcoming releases!

EDITOR **N.D. GRAY** once dreamed of being an astronaut. Now, she writes about characters who reach for the stars and fills their stories with magic, mayhem, and moolight.

When she's not writing, she works full time as a caregiver specializing in adults with I/DD, hangs out with the pup pack, and enjoys several creative pursuits, including acrylic painting.

Please visit her at ndgray.com

FOR MORE INFORMATION
PLEASE VISIT US AT
NDGRAY.COM/FAIRIESINJARS